The ZEITGEIST MACHINE

A New Anthology of
Science Fiction

The ZEITGEIST MACHINE

Selected by Damien Broderick

ANGUS & ROBERTSON PUBLISHERS

For Merv Binns
Secret Master of Aussie fandom

Angus & Robertson Publishers

London . Sydney . Melbourne . Singapore

Manila

First published by Angus & Robertson Publishers, Australia, 1977

© Damien Broderick 1977

National Library of Australia
card number and ISBN 0 207 13474 X

Printed in Hong Kong

CONTENTS

ACKNOWLEDGEMENTS

"The Inheritors" by G. M. Glaskin is reprinted by permission of the author and first appeared in "The Magazine of Fantasy and Science Fiction", New York, U.S.A., November 1972
© 1972 by G. M. Glaskin

Quotations throughout "Let it Ring" by John Foyster are from "The Underpeople" and "The Planet Buyer", by Cordwainer Smith. Reprinted by permission of Scott Meredith Literary Agency, Inc., 580 Fifth Avenue, New York, 10036, U.S.A.

"The Mountain Movers" by A. Bertram Chandler is reprinted by permission of the author and the author's agents, Scott Meredith Literary Agency, Inc.

"Growing up" by Damien Broderick first appeared in "Galileo", No. 1, September, 1976. Reprinted by permission of the author and the author's agent, Virginia Kidd.
© 1976 by Avenue Victor Hugo

"Conversations with Unicorns" is from *The Fat Man in History* by Peter Carey, reproduced by permission of University of Queensland Press

INTRODUCTION

Damien Broderick

Science fiction in Australia?

Why, yes. It burgeons and thrives. Melbourne has the Space Age Bookshop, run by fans, which specialises in the stuff. Sturdy display-racks elsewhere outmatch the porn lists, which aren't flagging either. Critics discuss sf on Lateline radio, devotees trek hundreds of kilometres each year to attend national sf conventions; in 1975 — *annus mirabilis*! — the prestigious World Science Fiction Convention itself, snatched like the Americas Cup from its traditional trustees, enlivened the Southern Cross Hotel.

This very book, the third Angus & Robertson science fiction anthology wholly by Australian authors, blips out a healthy ECG.

Australian science fiction?

Yes indeed. Warm-blooded, clawed and billed, it hatches and suckles its young, glides daringly from tall eucalyptus trees . . . Alas, it carries a Qantas ticket in its pouch.

After a pilgrimage to the Melbourne headquarters of the Guru Maharaj Ji, the writer Michael O'Rourke proposed that life is not like chocolate. I'm fairly sure he's mistaken. If not chocolate, life hereabouts is astonishingly like lamington. What follows are, admittedly, personal reflections. They relate specifically, however, to science

1

fiction, and Australia, and lamingtons; doubtless there are more general implications.

In 1971, freshly fired from my odious editorial position with this country's foremost tits and bums magazine, I was gladdened to read an unsolicited telegram from a large publishing house. In return for writing them a 15,000 word children's sf story, soon to be integrated lavishly with superior artwork, I would be given one thousand dollars. Here was a breakthrough!

With a little cry, I at once sat down and elaborated an idea I'd nibbled at some years earlier. The Pitjantjatjara aborigines, before they were hounded away from sacred Uluru (now the Ayers Rock Tourist Attraction), had recognised in that stone monolith a ferocious presence: the *wanambi*, the Rainbow Serpent. Oddly, it was their only myth bereft of animist rites.

Now suppose the *wanambi* were an alien being of prodigious power, penned in ages past beneath the Rock; suppose engineers stumbled on its Vault, and its defences, and were thrown back deranged; allow the possibility that a child's half-formed, flexible mind might cope with those defences to permit access . . . What archetypes of Abraham and Isaac might one explore, what resonance with everyday pain, and its repression, the gristle of each child's secret truth?

Well, in it went (grievously flawed, of course, for I had not previously written for children; I looked forward eagerly to dialogue with a smart editor), and in I went after it to see an unhappy gentleman. "What we really wanted," he said at last, "what we really had in mind, you see, was *Treasure Island on Mars*."

Several years later I was pleased to find in my letter-box an unsolicited telegram from a media production executive. His company after successful pilot programs on traditional (out-of-copyright) themes, planned a bold innovation: a "family viewing" science fiction series, utilizing sophisticated cartoon graphics.

I was naturally enchanted. Sf is a print-media phenomenon, yet it need not be: it is allusive, building worlds from hints, and the moving line is at once cheaper and less risky than huge sets, wooden actors and magnified toys. I pondered, and typed, and took my notion of an open-ended adventure series to the executive.

It posited an exhausted world, polluted and on its last gasp, and a megalomaniacal mission of survival experts frozen into the future in search of aid. If civilization did not perish outside their cryocapsules, its forms would grow increasingly bizarre with their every emergence into the unknowable future until finally some society mastered the time travel techniques required to return them home with the goodies — and, poignantly, abort their benefactors' history . . .

The executive nodded fretfully. Well, it was just an idea. He had been reading some sci-fi, he told me, by this fellow Asimov. That was really more what they had in mind. The Galactic History? Far out. No, no; what he actually wanted was, uh, like, *The Waltons on Mars*.

So, there's science fiction and there's sci fi. What of the true hard-core stuff in Australia?

Back in 1969, there was an exciting development for lovers of sf. A wealthy Australian businessman, who'd acquired an appetite for sf during the fabled Golden Age, announced the launching of a new magazine. Publishing exigencies precluded a purely Antipodean venture, so *VISION of Tomorrow* was to be edited from London, with an admixture of marsupial talent.

The magazine, I'm sorry to say, did not survive. A contributing factor was the informing vision of *VISION*'s Australian publisher: the magazine had been conceived principally to promote and reprint the works of a preposterous British hack who'd taken to the grave such pseudonyms as Vargo Statten and Volsted Gridban.

Australian science fiction? Sometimes the flow is blocked; sometimes it runs uphill to greener pastures; sometimes it gurgles into the sand and leaves little trace. David Rome, who wrote some excellent stories for John Carnell's *New Worlds*, is working in television and film. Jack Wodhams, a protege of *Analog*'s John W. Campbell, hailed by John Baxter as "undoubtedly the most promising

3

talent to emerge from Australian science fiction in its history'', has seen little work published since Campbell's death. Baxter himself, undoubtedly the most promising talent to emerge from Australian science fiction in its history, has apparently abandoned the genre for his other (and much more lucrative) interest, film criticisms. Several of the major ''fan'' critics and promoters of sf in Australia diligently cultivate their careers in preference to their avocation.

Science fiction in Australia? Let us, before passing on to the stories in this volume, brood a little longer on the matter, from a larger perspective:

Australians subsist, as everyone agrees, in a hand-me-down culture. It is of the essence of culture, admittedly, as much to be transmitted as to be renewed, but ours is curiously threadbare and ill-fitting. If a son asks for bread, the odds are high indeed that his father will give him a stone (or a lamington). It's an inevitable irony, then — and so, perhaps, no irony at all — that the world's finest science fiction to date was forged to a significant degree in the Australian experience. . .

. . . of an American writer, ''Cordwainer Smith''.

In May 1965, Smith's second collection of sf stories was published by Pyramid, a US paperback house. (Like Vonnegut's Kilgore Trout, the best sf writer in the world didn't crack it for hard-cover.) A month or two later I opened *Space Lords* and to my astonishment found in the Prologue: ''I know where I am. I'm right here in Canberra, A.C.T. — that's short for Australian Capital Territory, and we're a half day's run by motor to Sydney. The bank manager knows me, and the Church of England clergyman knows me, and you can even look in on Mr Greenish, my stockbroker, and ask him if my credit is good.''

Naturally, I packed a cheese sandwich and a change of socks in a large handkerchief slung on a stick, jumped the first turboprop from Melbourne to Canberra, and went out pink-eyed into the late afternoon to visit Mr. Greenish. I caught him just as his office was closing. With some dubiety he allowed that "Cordwainer Smith" must be Paul Linebarger, Ph. D., Certificate in Psychiatry (Applied), Litt. D., psychological warfare expert, until recently a visiting academic at the Australian National University but now, alas, on a field expedition somewhere in the Pacific.

One year later, Linebarger was dead. His friend Dr. Arthur Burns later recalled: "He (had been) constantly ill, usually with digestive or metabolic troubles, and had to put up with repeated surgery, so that in middle age he always lived close to the vital margin . . . He died while being prepared for a difficult and possibly not very hopeful operation, at the age of 54." So none of the fraternity of Australian sf enthusiasts ever had an opportunity to meet him. We knew him only through what his work told us of ourselves. And that was in the language of fairytale.

His last book was *Norstrilia*, about the boy Roderick Frederick Ronald Arnold William MacArthur McBann from the immensely rich world Old North Australia . . .

What was Norstrilia like?

Somebody once singsonged it up, like this:

"Gray lay the land, oh. Gray grass from sky to sky. Not near the weir, dear. Not a mountain, low or high — only hills and gray gray. Watch the dappled dimpled twinkles blooming on the star bar.

"That is Norstrilia . . .

"Beige-brown sheep lie on blue-gray grass while the clouds rush past, low overhead, like iron pipes ceilinging the world . . . "

It is incantatory stuff, taking us away from ourselves (if we know it) to bring us back. The critic John Foyster has noted: "He is talking to children; in his stories he is producing history as fairytales . . . This is not to demean, in any way, the intelligence or maturity of his readers; myths and legends have always been told in simple language . . . and to do otherwise would spoil much of their magic."

No Australian employing the multiple tongues of science fiction has written so well out of his native experience as

Linebarger did from several visits. Nor is it sufficient to retort that the genre is after all an instrument for amplifying American accents. It *is* that, but more deeply it's a transducer of the technological experience: the myth of the man/transistor interface. Our aspirations are linked ineluctably with the machine, with what the machine had done to and for us, and our world. We all press our mouths to the grease-nipple; for us, pity and terror are newly shaped, and can benefit from new means of expression.

So there have been attempts. They spring sometimes direct from the American vocabulary and syntax; sometimes from the electrical/chemical revival of *fin-de-siecle* voyage into sensory derangement; sometimes from the still-fruitful exercise of surrealist confrontation with irrational realities our bureaucratic enterprise would prefer to obliterate. Our second-hand culture may be dull, and anxious to remain dull, but the implosions and exhalations of radical change are seldom contained for long by the strictures of rule-book efficiency experts.

This may seem hazardous ground. Most pundits are quick to claim that the favourite reading matter of just such time-and-motion men is — science fiction. The issue is more complex, of course.

There was a certain justified song and dance a few years back about Norman Mailer's account of the first lunar landing, *A Fire On The Moon*. Due to an adolescence saturated in sf, my own response to that book was strangely skewed. Look, I'd girdled the galaxy when I was a kid, seen men's brains transplanted into devious bodies of cloned flesh, shared with time travellers the spectacle of Pleistocene and Omega Point.

How refreshing then, how heart-warming in its endlessly suggestive verisimilitude, was this rediscovered sf work from the late forties. Mailer's painstakingly devised terminology — surely the product of a mind bordering on compulsive obsession — made the lexicons of Robert Heinlein and Arthur C. Clarke threadbare indeed. And its

sociological leaps! Scarcely credible, on the face of it —
but suspend your disbelief and this rich kaleidoscope of a
possible 1969 A.D. will spring to life in your mind!

Alvin Toffler made much money not long ago by scaring
people with a deck of old sf concepts, cleverly shuffled
together with judicious quotes from incautious scientists,
capped with the admonition that reading sf was the
sovereign remedy and prophylactic for future shock.

Hmmm . . . He had a point, but it's rather like
advocating fornication on the grounds that the exercise
builds up your heart. In the thirties and forties certain dull
dogs went a similar route, recommending sf as a
sugar-coated pill which would fire young minds with
enthusiasm for laboratory careers. In the event, the Cold
War did that rather more efficiently; we are now suffering
its success.

Then Kingsley Amis came along at the end of the fifties,
doing his bit to coax the flashy slattern in off the streets.
Science fiction was, he informed us, a satirical medium, a
mirror for our woes, an arena for expressing dissent in a
blandly repressive society. New maps of hell. Maps of
new hells.

It was a valuable codification of some things sf writers
and readers had always known about the genre. But
partial. Sf stories, in truth, are new maps of hell *and*
heaven *and* earth. Sf stories are games. Fairytales for
adults.

If that still seems derogatory, it's because there's been
too much badmouthing of fairytales. Biologists of the
holist school recognise a process termed *neoteny*: the
carry-over into adulthood by a new species of some
valuable infantile characteristic of the old. It has been
argued that neoteny split Man off from his primate
forebears. Man is a neotenized chimpanzee — what a
superchimp foetus would grow up into if it didn't turn into
an ape.

The evolutionary moral seems to be that a certain
amount of childishness does an adult a lot of good. It's a
terrible shame when you lose your love of fairytales. But

7

what can you do? Well, fortunately, there's science fiction. Fairytales for adults.

Games can be viewed as the way kids learn the ins and outs of social interaction, discover the values of assertion and co-operation, test and develop a whole range of skills. But don't tell a child that. He'll think you're crazy. He knows he plays games because they're *fun*.

Some sociologists have built entire models of the adult world on the concept of games. *Homo ludens*: that's us. Games are formal structures of behaviour with a certain permissible variety of gambit and counter-move within a specified frame of goals, payoffs (and sometimes penalties). The richer the structure, the more fun the game is. You're never through playing games: you just get bored with the simple ones, and ask for something more demanding and rewarding.

Science fiction is a literary game that — more or less accurately, often honouring the exploratory spirit rather than the stringent letter — filches from science a playing field of galaxies and a set of rules defined by what we know or would like to discover about the way the universe ticks.

Like all good games, the rules must not be broken — unless an amusing and plausible loop hole can be found. The sf writer's job is to startle and amaze his readers by whipping unexpected — but not gratuitous — bunnies out of the hat. In the doing of it he may instruct, warn, proselytize, mock, and even provide sneaky Rorschach blots — but that's not what you're paying him for.

So, pre-eminently, science fiction is play for the zest of it. If it rarely attains the stature of high art, that is doubtless because its intentions are more modest. It is a literature of entertainment. It displays wonders for our astonishment and delight.

Yet that limited brief need not render a genre trivial, nor entail an abdication from moral seriousness. If a writer means to lead us on a romp, we ought not rebuke him for failing to initiate us into the numinous. Sometimes, though, sf passes from titillation through ravishment to awe, and when it does it can move us (because of the concerns which specify its games) into an exploration of dimensions that ordinarily elude us.

Let me return for a moment to Cordwainer Smith, whose sf (until the advent of Thomas Disch, Ursula Le Guin and perhaps Samuel Delany and Joanna Russ) came closest to art. Dr. Arthur Burns, in a tribute in *Australian Science Fiction Review*, tells us:

"Smith's stories were a kind of important 'playing' — through them are dotted irrelevant cryptograms, geographic allusions, and names transliterated from foreign languages. He once said that Cordwainer Smith was a 'pre-Cervantean' — the stories are like cycles of medieval legends, without the Aristotelian beginning-middle-and-end of classic tragedy, and certainly without the same structure as transposed into the modern novel, which Cervantes began. They are legendary cycles of the future, rather than future history, and were meant to be connected with and consistent with each other on the legendary and not the historiographical model . . . evocations of the emotional and imaginative responses of people in bizarre social relationships and situations. . ."

Such "playing" reminds us most of Jorge Luis Borges — yet one could hardly approach Borges with the same expectation of simple pleasure which, when Cordwainer Smith was alive, gladdened the readers of *Galaxy*. It is instructive that there is no university syllabus of literature in which Cordwainer Smith's works can be found listed next to Borges' . . .

Since this is a collection of sf and fantasy stories by Australian writers, Dr. Linebarger's crucial contribution to our sf cannot, alas, be represented. Yet his influence is not absent. John Foyster's "Let It Ring" is explicitly a tribute to "the old poet": a dense, multi-layered story which comes closest of these tales to the "new wave" of non-conventional subject and treatment in sf.

At one level, it exemplifies the curious paradox that sf is often a parochial, self-referring genre, for all its galactic pretensions: the powerplays mockingly echo Australian "sf fandom's" manoeuvres to bring the World SF Convention here in 1975, climaxing at the Toronto Convention of 1973 where the bid proved successful.

At another, it is the dream of a contemporary movie director, whose fantasy of a distant future slowly gives way to languid awakening, and sex with his mistress. Startlingly, the truly sf element is the awareness of that dream's protagonist that he is a figure in a dream (of a movie, in a short story . . . ?) And for all this elaboration, the tale vividly conveys an appreciation, too rarely found in massive galactic epics, of the dismal issues underlying the imperial dialectic.

At an extreme remove is Lee Harding's "Spaceman". The dislocation of consciousness he examines is as old as the bitter rift between ancient nomad pastoralists and their Ur-urban cousins; as thoroughly grounded in narrative tradition as any tale of a ship's crewman gone missing to the lure of tropic idyll. Is it, then, in any sense, peculiarly Australian? I think so.

We are, on the whole, raw, vulgar; our communal tastes lack any hint of genuine cultivation. We excuse this coarseness by appeal to "bush mateship", a pragmatics of social accord rendered in a crucible of harsh geography, scant resources, the root-severing distance from Europe.

All this special pleading is, of course, mendacious. Last time I looked at the figures, we were the most urbanized culture on earth: 86 percent of the population in cities, suburbs, largish towns. Electronic communication grids us so uncompromisingly into the globe that in one recent notorious epiphany the Australian public was told of important US military plans before the President managed to inform his American constituency. We are, if anything, the victims of technological triumph. If the bush once spoke to our shearers and poets, its voice is now hardly audible over the crash and screech of process-line, office equipment, television commercials, overpowered motor cars and jet-lagged impresarios. We are the spacemen of Harding's story.

It is the machine-genie's stunning success in making and sustaining our cultural matrix which informs Dal Stivens' "The Wonderfully Intelligent Sheepdog", and which persuaded me to select it in preference to one of his urbane sf stories from *Fantastic Universe.* Stivens is a man of many parts, but he is superbly a fabulist. His surreal cameos are as close to Aesop as to baccy-stained tall bush yarns. But his miraculous sheepdog, one sees, is in fact the sf robot in shaggy disguise. Rather, the adroit mutant, strange kin to Cordwainer Smith's animal-derived Underpeople. Nor, on internal evidence, is "Sheepdog" a fantasy — clearly, the *mise en scene* is a region graced with peculiar scientific properties, a sort of outback Bermuda Triangle . . .

A locale skewed still more oddly is the setting for Michael Wilding's "Illumination". In John Baxter's *Australian Science Fiction 2,* Wilding gave us a haunting account of the "man of slow feeling", a victim of a mind/body split evocative of our own more quotidian malaise. Now he approaches the same theme even more starkly, clinically coaxing sensory disruption into the realm of ontological crisis.

I have argued that our supposed bush heritage is thin pottage indeed. Yet such images, if repeated often enough (as they are), have a power to stir us in spite of distance. G. M. Glaskin's "The Inheritors" works with one such utterly Australian image to create authentic horror in the soul of the most obdurate high-rise tenant. His technique in this tale deftly captures the genuine ham-handedness of traditional Australian writing — a style characterised by one overseas observer as "jejune to the point of slap-happy". It is wickedly ingenious that his bathetic protagonist is presented as a popular novelist (a role enjoyed by Glaskin himself).

If Australia has, in all truth, no great density of science fiction tradition, it does possess writers ready to penetrate adjacent realms. Until very recently, though, this step has been thought unnecessarily bold. When Thomas Keneally's *A Dutiful Daughter* was released by Penguin in

1972, the publishers edged up to the question of proprieties by announcing it as "an act of exceptional and provocative imagination, an authentic specimen of the new fiction which is not content merely to reproduce realities but insists on making them up". Peter Carey is a young writer who, working in that territory as though it were the most natural thing in the world, managed (quite justly) to elicit squeals of delight from all corners when his *The Fat Man In History* came out in 1974. "Conversations With Unicorns" is from that collection.

A similar surreal pungency marks Stephen Cook's "The Kitten". Its excellence, alas, is cause for pain, a reminder of possibilities expunged; Stephen Cook died by his own hand in 1967.

Making up realities need not, of course, compel us into unfamiliar inner voids and spaces. A. Bertram Chandler is our most industrious sf writer, winner of three Ditmar awards (an annual presentation for merit awarded by Australian sf aficionados). Of his "All Laced Up", in *Australian Science Fiction 1*, John Baxter noted: "To the science fiction writer, anything is grist to the mill. Even the simplest object can be made the basis of a story." Or, in the case of "The Mountain Movers", the most commonplace vacation.

In a reminiscence entitled "My Life and Grimes" (the redoubtable Grimes being a serial protagonist whose career in the Rim Worlds parallels remarkably his creator's), Captain Chandler revealed that the story was born in a bus tour through the Dead Heart. That strange landscape, echoing only to myths we whites have exterminated, clearly presented the aspect of an alien world . . .

No less haunted and alien, I dare say, is the world of publishing where off-beat stories like these must find their home. Lacking indigenous sf magazines, the Australian fantasy writer must look to overseas markets (with their xenophobic restrictions on setting, idiom, and point of central concern), the marginal literary periodicals, and the local mass-circulation magazines.

The latter, with their horrid insistence on banality and cretin-level accessibility, are so close to a fate worse than death that our few fantasists have largely passed by on the other side. "Incubation", written by playwright John Romeril and I in 1966, is an exception to that rule; that it was later reprinted in *VISION of Tomorrow* suggests that it meets more specialized tastes as well. Because we were writing for a local men's magazine, Romeril and I set out to exploit and satirize (immanently, as it were) precisely the bizarre shibboleths of that strangled idiom. Oddly enough, I think our story turned up some small additional increment of serendipitous virtue.

Due to such dismal constraints, Cherry Wilder's splendid tale "Point of Departure" appears here in print for the first time. Wilder is new to science fiction, but it is clear that her talent will bring her glory. With a limpid, evocative grace, she here introduces a forth-coming series of stories about the marsupial Moruia of Torin. Like the superb Ursula Le Guin, she is an sf writer who can feel as well as think, and her quiet words let us see what she sees: something new, marvellous, rewarding.

In short: eleven stories of fantasy and science fiction by Australians, each refracting after its particular fashion some single hue from our distinctive experience.

Enjoy, enjoy.

One last lamington as envoi.

During the preparation of this anthology, I contacted the University of Queensland Press to obtain copyright release for one of these tales. Now the U.Q.P. is a body I regard with admiration, respect and gratitude, for of late it has ventured into areas of fresh, experimental prose where more commercial publishers have dared not tread. Imagine my pleasure when a U.Q.P. editor, in his reply, presented this unsolicited invitation:

"The thought occurred to me that there should be something published . . . on the place of science fiction in contemporary literature . . . (perhaps less 'speedy' and catalogue-like than [Brian Aldiss'] *The Billion Year Spree*) . . ."

It happened that for some little time I had been preparing just such a volume, culling local and overseas sources for the best pieces of lively and/or densely-argued literary criticism in the field: structural analysis by Poland's polymathic Stanislaw Lem, Kuhnian paradigmatics by Alexei Panshin, the "cognitive estrangement" hypothesis of Professor Darko Suvin, the aesthetics of Franz Rottensteiner, and sundry dazzling probes by Chip Delany, George Turner, John Foyster and others.

In a flash I dispatched the Ms. to St Lucia, 4067, praising God that at last the scholarly community might reap the benefit of the patient, persistent toil of three Australian enthusiasts — John Bangsund, Bruce Gillespie and John Foyster — in whose "fanzines" much of the work had first appeared, or first been available in English.

Well, it was all a mistake, and no-one is to blame. Back it came.

" . . . the collection as it stands . . . too thoroughly part of the committed world of science fiction readership to win over the kind of sceptical or uninitiated audience I have in mind . . . fairly drastic cuts to . . . over-esoteric material . . . more accessible to the uninitiated reader . . .

Yes, of course it was a mistake, and what they had in mind was a persuasive primer; at the very most, *The Common Pursuit on Mars*. But there's that faint tickling giggle at the back of my pineal gland speculating on the prevalence, in University Presses around the world, of rejection on the basis of *esotericism*, for Christ's sake.

"Dear sir,

"We thoroughly enjoyed your 'Phenomenological Poetics of Brecht's *Verfremdung*', but from the point of view of publication the work is flawed by your gratuitous assumption that the theatre is worthy of attention, and made doubly arduous for the ordinary reader by your covert assumption that he ought be conversant with the dramaturge's actual writings. The Ms. is returned under separate cover." There's pavlova stuck in my teeth.

Science fiction in Australia?

We're getting there (the scent of a primer, after all, is the early morning promise of a bright noon); and indeed, haven't I been insisting that sf is primarily a literature of entertainment?

The stories are waiting. Bon appetit!

DAMIEN BRODERICK

THE INHERITORS

G. M. Glaskin

For some of humanity — even if it *is* a very small section of it compared with the rest of the world — the first mention of it all was an item of only a few inches on (already a bad augury?) page 13 of Perth's morning newspaper, *The West Australian*. It read:

FARMER MAULED

Farmer Victor E. Timms (47) of West Wyanilling collapsed unconscious from his vehicle which he had managed to drive 8 miles from his property to Wyanilling township after having received severe wounds to most of his body from savage mauling, presumably by wild dogs. He was taken by ambulance to the Narrogin District Hospital where his condition was said to be serious. At the time of this report, Mr. Timms, who lived alone on his property, had not regained consciousness to inform the investigating police officer as to where and by what he had been attacked.

I suppose the newspaper report is near enough to what must have happened, but what I wasn't at all sure about even then was the wild dogs bit. I mean, I know there are any amount of dingoes in Australian countryside, and they were known to be savage enough when cornered or their young were being endangered. But by the look of that unfortunate farmer — and all four of us had had all too good a look — there had been several more than just the one dingo which had attacked him, if only by the number of bites all over his body and the way his clothes were ripped to shreds so that there wasn't much of his body left unexposed.

Yet dingoes don't usually roam in packs; they're mostly loners. Also, having spent some time in wheatbelt country during my lifetime, I thought I knew a dingo bite when I saw one, or just an ordinary dog's bite for that matter. And these bite marks hadn't at all looked like those from any kind of canine to me, not unless they had indeed been made by just the one animal and that particular animal had lost all of its upper front teeth.

For that was what had been so peculiar about the hideous wounds on farmer Timms when we reached him; each wound showed teeth marks where the flesh had been ripped away, but only on the one side of the wound. On the other side of it the skin was still left attached to the body, though bruised and torn of course. But there was no laceration or even a puncture mark on this upper side of the wound.

There were no dogs, wild or otherwise, that I knew of with natural mouth formations like this. This meant that if the wounds had indeed been made by a mouth with the upper front teeth missing, there must have been only the one animal; it would be too much of a coincidence for two of them — let alone more, no matter what they had been — to have had the same upper front teeth all missing. And yet if there *had* been only the one, why hadn't Timms been able to fend it off? How could even one dog, again wild or not, overcome a grown and able man by itself?

But of course we weren't ever to know what had happened to Timms on his West Wyanilling property that Saturday afternoon, for he never recovered consciousness before dying in just a little over forty-eight hours afterwards. A bachelor, he'd lived alone on his property; so there was no one else either to have seen what had happened. But then, like most things, the apprehension aroused by this gruesome tragedy had soon died and been forgotten.

But that wasn't the only event that day which left us all with a very nasty sort of sensation that, for a while at

17

least, was pretty well akin to fear, I should say — even terror.

I've already said there were the four of us, and so I'd better elaborate. There was a local interest in the possibility of filming one of my novels set in that part of the country, and so the four of us — Bill Cousins and his wife, Jo, or Joanna, and Beryl and myself — had driven down the 120 miles or so southwest from the city of Perth to see if the township of Wyanilling was still much as I had described it in a novel written over ten years before. It was almost *completely* unchanged, which didn't at all surprise me for that part of the country; it doesn't have the rest of the world's almost hysterical *need* to change. Even the pub was pretty much as it had been ten years before, and as I had described it in my book. Moreover, all of the local setting — from Wyanilling clean into the city of Perth 120 miles away — had shown very little change either. The film could be made with very little studio work, which would mean an almost unbelievably economical production budget.

And this is what, in a way, we'd been celebrating, the four of us, with a few beers for Bill and me and brandy crusters for the girls, in the very pub where we expected to be shooting film in the not too distant future. We were just about finished and deciding to move off when we'd heard the shouts and noises of alarm outside, and like everyone else in the pub we rushed out to see what was happening.

Even the drinks didn't really help us to get over the shock of seeing Timms and the state he'd been in. He'd come swerving his vehicle down the street and straight towards us, only swinging it over at the very last minute; we still had to jump for it to miss us. Then his driving door had wrenched open and he'd come flying out — to be hurled bleeding spread-eagled along the road. He'd come to rest almost at our feet, and my *God*, he'd been in a mess.

But I've already told you about that. By this time it was getting near five, and so we thought we ought to start getting back to the city and dinner somewhere.

We'd gone only a few miles when Bill suddenly pulled up on a narrow and rather deserted piece of road before we had reached the main highway. As far as I could see, there was nothing but empty and barren paddocks with a few parched-looking trees here and there. There weren't even any stock — sheep, I mean — in sight. Yet Bill was getting out his 16mm camera and mounting it into its harness.

"Gawd! What you going to shoot here, Bill!" his wife, Jo, wanted to know. She'd just had her brandy crusters severely jerked, for one thing; and I suppose the shock of the savaged farmer hardly left her in the mood for absorbing, let along filming, some of the local scenery. In any case, it all looked pretty awful hereabouts. This wasn't surprising. As it was in about the worst state it had ever been known to be in, after the longest and severest drought yet recorded.

Bill was almost apologetic as he stood spread-eagled a few feet off from the car and aimed and focused his camera.

"I need a few fill-in shots for a telly commercial," he said. He spoke almost as though he was being obliged to film some shots at a funeral. The camera whirred; then he moved off a few feet more, then another few feet, so that we all decided we might as well stretch our legs a bit, seeing we'd be about two hours getting back to the city; and once started, no doubt Bill wouldn't want to stop again till we got there. In any case, Joanna wanted to go behind a tree, she said; and so Beryl thought she'd better go with her. I can remember shouting something bawdy about not falling in, or something like that, more to break the mood of despondency which, very understandably, had set in on us after Timms. I went off in another direction and then over to see what on earth — what on all this so *parched* earth around us — Bill could be finding to photograph.

"Nothing much," he said. "But it's just what I need — a jolly good stretch of parched earth!" As though to illustrate his point, he even kicked up a few clods with his dust-covered boots and took some C.U.'s (sorry, close-ups) of the dust he'd kicked up as it went drifting off on the cool but so lifeless evening air. It's a dreadful thing to see, a country in drought.

The girls were just returning from the other side of the road when Bill remarked to me about how he wished there had been at least a *few* sheep left around even though he knew it was damned near impossible for them to survive in the country as reduced as it was now. Most of the farmers had taken them to the abattoirs weeks before — or else had bulldozed the carcasses by the thousand into huge open graves they'd had to dig and then fill in again. We'd passed I don't know how many dams which normally didn't even need to be used at this time of the year; there was usually plenty of crop for feed, and water. But even the dams were dried out, cracked hard, like they usually are at the end of summer.

"Just a few sheep scratching up the dust in all this is all I need," Bill said.

It was almost uncanny the way they came, just as if they'd heard him.

The girls saw them first. They'd both come up behind us, Jo shading her eyes against the last of the evening sun rays. Suddenly she pointed to the top of the hill where there was a dense clump of trees sticking out gaunt and stark against the green-gold skyline.

"Aren't those some sheep up *there*," she said, squinting.

And then we all saw them.

They were coming down slowly, very slowly, from the top of the hill, from out of that stark clump of gaunt dry trees that looked propped against the seared skyline. We might never have seen them if they hadn't been pointed out to us by Joanna; they were coated in dust and so were the same color as the dusty earth all around them. And they were moving so slowly that it might have been no more than a faint shadow moving across the earth with the last of the fast-setting sun. The most distinguishable thing about them was the dust they managed to stir up and set drifting off away from them, like a long low veil across the dust-colored earth. Even the sky was dust-colored.

"Yeah," Bill said, "they're sheep all right. But it'll be midnight before they make it down here, at the rate they're going. Unless I go up there to meet them. But I'm afraid I don't feel up to it. Oh, well! Too bad! They might have made a *few* good shots . . ."

"That's funny," Beryl said.

"What?" I asked her.

"They've stopped."

"So they have," said Jo.

And they had. The cloud of dust was already drifting away from them. Then it started up again.

"No, they're coming on again," Bill said.

And they were. And once again it was pretty uncanny, as though they had not only materialized out of the dust and parched air, but now, just for Bill's sake, were getting energy from God knows where to stir themselves up into a kind of jog, then a trot, then a canter. And then, by God, they were suddenly — the whole lot of them — fair galloping towards us.

"Oh, you bloody little beauties!" Bill said enthusiastically, and soon had the camera whirring away.

It was amazing how they came down that hill. I don't suppose I shall ever forget it, even though I didn't at all know then, of course, what we all too grimly know now. It was almost like a landslide, an avalanche, the sheep the same dust-color as the parched earth all around them.

"I don't understand it!" Joanna was saying. "They usually run *away* from you, not *towards* you!"

"That's what *I* thought!" Beryl said.

I had to agree.

"Not since the drought," Bill told us, still working hard on his camera.

"How do you mean?" I asked him.

"They're being *hand*-fed, and hand-*watered* — those of 'em that are still alive."

"So?"

"Well, it only stands to reason, doesn't it? As soon as they see a vehicle these days — almost *any* kind of vehicle, I suppose — they think it means food and water, so they head straight for it. See? Just like they're doing now. Come on, you little beauties, you! Come on for Daddy Bill!"

And his camera went on whirring with his hand deftly zooming the lens in and out.

"Gawd!" he said after another moment or two. "I couldn't have got it better if I'd tried!"

It was an incredible sight, now that all those sheep were so much closer to us — close enough, now, to see the ribs sticking out through their wool, their thin sticks of legs. Some of them, poor bastards, must have fallen and ripped skin from themselves, and the flies had blown them. Even without that, they stank.

"My God!" Jo suddenly cried out. "Aren't they going to *stop* !"

I must say it looked as though they weren't. Bill was the only one on the other side of the fence, and he soon decided that all the film in the world wasn't worth being stampeded by a flock of frantic sheep. I've never seen him move so quickly as he did then, camera and all, vaulting the fence and hotfooting it back to the car. I think all four doors opened pretty well simultaneously, and all four of us felt considerably safer behind the frail enough protection which is all that a modern-style car can offer — little more than cardboard-thick metal and only slightly thicker glass. All the same, it did manage to give at least *some* consolation.

For a moment I thought the sheep were going to come at us clean through the fence. Or even *over* it. I wasn't the only one. Joana gave a little involuntary cry, and suddenly I could feel Beryl shaking against me.

But then, thank God, they did stop, though I feel sure it was only the fence that had stopped them. Even then, a good many of those in the front were still being pushed towards us by those at the back. I've never really studied sheep from close up before, and I suppose they were hardly sheep we were all gaping back at now, they were so emaciated from the drought. But what struck me more than anything this time was their eyes, so rounded and red from being bloodshot, and at the same time quite dilated, as though from fear — or perhaps fearsomeness?

Bill was saying, "They think we've brought water for them, all right — the poor bastards! God, look at the way their mouths drool! And their tongues hang out!"

It was true. Some of them did drool, a kind of sticky mess that looked more solid than liquid as though there wasn't enough liquid left in their bodies to form saliva. I didn't want to look at them much longer; I don't suppose any of us did. I could still feel Beryl shaking, and crying too now, beside me.

"God, it's awful!" she said quietly. I could feel her nails biting into my arm.

Jo was saying, "I don't want to look at them any longer, Bill. For God's sake get us out of here!"

So he did.

I think the sight of those sheep had upset us even more than what they had almost made us forget — the savaged body of farmer Timms.

If we had thought that this was going to be the end of horrors for the day, then we were mistaken. Just before reaching the highway, we had to cross the railway line going south to Albany. There's probably only the one train a day — well, passenger train anyway, and admittedly this was a freight train — but *we* had to strike it. So we were held up at the crossing for about three minutes or so, three minutes we could all have done very well without.

It was Beryl who saw these other few sheep, just a few yards away from us in a corner of yet another parched paddock where the road and railway line and paddock fence all met together. There were only five or six of them, mostly full grown — if you could apply the term 'fully grown' to animals which were emaciated to almost half their normal size. But one of them was only a lamb — or rather it had been. I don't know whether it had been killed by some other means, or whether the grown sheep had killed it, though I'd never heard of sheep killing other sheep and nor do I know anyone who has. But whatever happened to that lamb, the rest of them were making short work of it, rending it with their bloodied mouths while their small, almost sinisterly delicate little cloven hoofs pounded and pounded at the now-battered body beneath them. I could have sworn they were drinking the lamb's blood, as no doubt they were. Was it possible, with this horrifying drought, that they had turned not only killers but cannibals as well?

I was almost tempted to get out of the car to go and look to find out, but the train had rumbled on past us; and before I could say anything, Bill was driving on again. In any case, Joanna had now seen them, and she suddenly cried out, "Oh, Christ! They're even killing them*selves*, now — to eat and drink!"

I'd hoped Jo wouldn't have seen, for I hadn't wanted Beryl to see it. As we drove on I felt her suddenly wrench, retching, beside me; but she did manage not to vomit. All the same, I wished she hadn't seen it. On the other hand, I couldn't help thinking to myself how it had been known in similar times of stress for even human beings to hack and rend each other, to eat their own kind's flesh, and drink their own kind's blood. So why not sheep? Lord knows, they have little enough brains . . .

And there's all the Biblical stuff, of course — that also, now comes to mind:

Blood of the lamb, pray for us . . .

Sacrificial lambs all through the Bible, all through the ages.

Blood of the lamb, wash away our sins . . .

And Abraham about to sacrifice Isaac, his only son, but then had instead taken a lamb, wasn't it? — and slit *its* throat instead. Which I suppose *had* been a little more humane of him.

Blood of the lamb, wash away the sins of our fathers . . .

And in a way I suppose they still do go to be sacrificed.

But not just one at a time, now. By the hundreds. The thousands. All being led to the slaughter. I've heard them at the abattoirs, being herded bleating to each other along the pens and up the ramps to the hammer that, mercifully, does give them a belt on the top of the head before they're slaughtered, then skinned and drawn to be freighted off and then dissected ready for our dining tables . . .

And once — and only the once, thank God — I've seen them brought in for shearing, sheep reared for their wool instead of their flesh. You'd think that would be so much better, wouldn't you? But if you do, then you couldn't be more wrong. It's worse. Much worse. I don't think I've ever seen anything quite so horrible, even though I well know it's the kind of inhuman cruelty which really *is* being kind.

It's called 'crutching' — and it's done on the young lambs when they're brought in for the first time. Wool and excrement just don't go together very well, and so their tails have to be lopped off. Well, that isn't so bad, you might think, and neither it is. They just bleed and probably hurt for a short while, and that, you would think, would be that. But not so. There is still all the wool that grows long and thick all around their hindquarters, and this, too, gets in the way of their excrement. It sticks to the wool and then gradually accumulates. And in Australia there are always the bush flies; no matter where you are or what time of year it may be, you can never manage to escape the Australian bush flies. And these feed on anything, especially excrement. So they alight and feed on the excrement accumulated on the young sheep's backsides and then 'blow' it, or lay their eggs in it, and out hatch the maggots to feed on it in turn. Only the maggots don't stop at just the excrement; they eat down to the flesh and then into it. To hear a young sheep bleating because it is being eaten alive is almost as agonizing as anything I've heard.

But I've also heard them bleating to make the sky quake when they've been submitted to the prophylactic treatment which is all that, so far, man has devised for them. Not only the tail is lopped off; they're upended on a kind of rack, say half a dozen at a time, with a man standing behind each lamb, each man with a knife. The knife makes a deft and circular cut, without anaesthetic, all around the sheep's anus for about the size of a saucer. Then the skin is wrenched off to leave the raw and bleeding flesh — about the size of a saucer, remember — which is then daubed with an antiseptic.

When they're released, they can do nothing but stand in their agony and bleat till you'd think they'd bleat their pathetic hearts out. I was standing on a sheep station at the time when I saw and heard this for myself. When nightfall came, they didn't stop. I had a bit of a respite from them when we were all inside for dinner, but only till the time came for me to leave my host and hostess and go over to the quarters they had kindly lent me for the two or three days I had intended staying there. As soon as I was outside, my ears were immediately smitten with those pitiful cries again. I couldn't help it, I lay awake listening to them. They were somehow all the more horrifying at night. I thought I'd never sleep. Yet I did; I did. But I also had the most horrifying dream. Instead of this operation being performed on mere sheep (and note how one mammalian animal, man, can think of another as 'mere'), I dreamt that it was being performed, like circumcision perhaps, on small children. Even babies. No, I should think by the tone of the cries I heard in this nightmare that they could have been *only* babies. Anyway, I remember waking up from it in the middle of the night with a severe shock of horror.

It was even more horrifying to find that the *dream* might have ended, but the cries still continued. And my God, how like babies they sounded. Indeed, it took me a few moments before I could bring myself to realize that they *weren't* babies. They were just *sheep*, I had to tell myself. *Just sheep . . .*

On the other hand, cruel as this may seem, you have to see the alternative for yourself, those flyblown and then maggot-ridden rumps, and hear the cries of agony that then come from the sheep to know what greater cruelty the alternative is. And it was God who devised *that* one. All the same, with all his science and anaesthetics, analgesics and things, you'd think that man could devise something at least a *little* less inhuman than *that* sort of treatment . . .

Blood of the lamb
Pray for us!
Blood of the lamb
Wash away our sins!
Blood of the lamb
Wash away the sins of our fathers . . .

I don't know why, I can only suppose that because I had seen Timms in Wyanilling almost three weeks before, but when a second farmer — or, rather, a farmhand this time — met a similar fate in another outlying township of the wheat and sheep district, I felt compelled to go and see this victim as well. I had an almost proprietorial feeling about it, or attitude towards it. Not only that, but it was almost a sense of civic duty that compelled me to drive — alone this time — to East Dowernup where this second savaging had been reported.

This time the victim had already died by the time I got there. There had to be an autopsy, of course, but there was no actual morgue as such in so small a community. But because of the nature of the fatality, the police didn't want the body removed to a larger town which did have the proper facilities. So the body was accommodated in the freezer of the local butcher. Appropriate fate, it occurred to me, for someone who had earned his living all his life breeding and rearing thousands upon thousands of other beings for exactly the same fate, with the addition of at least being spared the consumption of his own carcass by being eaten afterwards.

I thought I was going to be denied seeing the body, even in my capacity of a novelist using the pretext of wanting to see a body after such an attack for a possible future or even present work. The policeman on duty, and possibly quite rightly so, wouldn't have a bar of it. It was only when I divulged to him that I had seen the body, though before death had occurred on that occasion, of farmer Timms who had died similarly that he finally relented. Even then it was mainly because, I could easily see, the policeman thought he might be able to obtain some information and details which, it was even more obvious, were defying his powers of intelligence over this particular demise.

They were the same kind of marks precisely. Whatever had killed this young farmhand of not quite nineteen had possessed the same kind of mouth as that which had killed farmer Timms; there were no teeth-marks left from the upper jaw of the mouth; but only the bruising and slight tearing of flesh as before. A mortician had not been called in to the body, of course, and so the dead face still bore the same terrible expression of horror and agony with which he had died. I was almost tempted to close his staring eyes myself, with the tips of two fingers, as I had seen so often done in films, if never in reality, and then to smooth away the terrible expression of agony and horror with the back or curve of my hand, as I had again seen done in films but never in reality. It was almost as though I had the feeling that the dead youth would not be able to rest in the peace so many of us seem to expect for ourselves on that other side of this life — not until such time as his agony and horror had been smoothed away from his features, so permitting them to assume an appropriate arrangement, and therefore suggestion of repose.

But I did restrain myself. And when I pointed out the peculiar nature of the bite marks to the policeman, it did at least compel him to push back his cap and then scrape and scratch at that part of his head where it was obvious that a bald patch would not be long in appearing. He was also compelled to remark, "Yeah, I see what you mean. Makes you think, don't it!"

But that, of course, is precisely, perhaps because of incapability, what he didn't do.

"Too small a bite to have been a bull or anything like that," he did manage to derive, still continuing with his scratching and scraping. "Don't know what else it could have been — 'cept maybe one of them dingo bastards, with some of his upper teeth missing . . .''

But I, of course — like you long before this now, I trust — already had my suspicions, incredible as they might seem.

You'd never believe it, but I asked no less than five farmers who had been sheep farming for the better part if not all of their lives, and not one of those five could tell me what the inside of a sheep's mouth looked like. Some weeks later, at an agricultural show, I made yet another attempt and found that the first three I asked also hadn't the faintest idea. But sheep were being judged for prize giving, sheep which had been given what you might call almost a 'hothouse' looking-after, being the prize specimens they were. To be judged, they had to be inspected. And part of that inspection was the forcible opening of tneir jaws, with their quarters held firmly between the judge's own legs, for inspection of teeth and gums.

And so I was able to verify the matter for myself, despite having already looked it up in the *Encyclopedia Britannica*. Sheep have a full set of teeth in the bottom jaw, but there is only a long bony structure at the top front, like an external projection of the upper jaw, replacing what otherwise might have been four or perhaps even six upper teeth, such as most other mammals have, even that other herbivorous animal, the horse.

It seemed incredible, yet it was such a logical explanation — especially when, in the next few days, no less than six other men, two women and a child, were to die in exactly the same horrible way. All had obviously been taken by surprise, although by now the whole rural countryside was keeping an unrelenting lookout for even the slightest sign of wild dogs or dingoes, or even just the one lone animal for that matter. How, then, had the victims been taken by surprise? It now seemed obvious to me — because their killer had been an animal which normally they wouldn't have even the slightest suspicion to fear. Who had ever been attacked at all, let alone fatally, by the gentle and, if anything, quite stupid sheep?

Gentle and quite stupid?

The next disaster was an entire family — the parents and five children aged from a youth of seventeen to a baby girl of not quite two. None had survived. Moreover they had been dead and, worst horror of all, partly devoured for two or three days when they were found, and only then by their failure to answer an operator-handled instead of an automatic telephone.

The police found no footprints from dogs of any kind, though the farmhouse was surrounded by those from sheep, even though the sheep were, by the time of the discovery, some distance away from the farmhouse again.

This time, or so I was assured by the police officer in charge, all the bodies were much too disfigured to have mere bite marks discerned. Just about all the bulky part of their flesh, he told me, had been torn from the skeletons. Even the cheeks and limbs, the ears, had been eaten away — and especially the soft parts of the throat. The woman's breasts and the buttocks of all the victims had been eaten clean away. Some of the bones of the victims had been cracked and fractured, as though submitted to a relentless pummeling by some smallish but hard and perhaps even sharp objects. And I was immediately reminded of the smallish yet hard and sharp appearance of the sheep's hoof.

It might have occurred to me that it was sheep, driven in their dementia for food and drink, which were the savage killers of, by now, just under twenty people; but it certainly didn't seem to have occurred to anyone else. Or if it had, then no one had said anything about it. I suppose it was, as it had at first seemed to me, much too incredible. I even wrote a letter to *The West Australian* about it, but they declined to publish it, saying they had conferred on the matter with agricultural experts who had all disputed my suggestion, although admittedly having no other explanation to offer. I wrote again when yet another entire family and the three hired helpers they employed had all been found dead and partly devoured in and around the farmhouse. This time they must have been attacked in daylight instead of in their sleep as the first family had been, for a farmhand and two of the children who performed some of the lighter duties around the property had been found torn to pieces in the paddocks. The woman and two more of her six children had managed to escape the house, only to be overwhelmed within short distances from it. But even this second letter was returned to me with nothing more than the customary "the editor regrets" slip.

It was now no longer the bleating of sheep which tormented me; it was the so much more hideous screams of their victims.

"Baa, baa black sheep, have you any wool?"

"Yes, sir! Yes, sir! Three bags full!"

I tried the agricultural department myself, and now I wish I hadn't. Even a layman shouldn't be inflicted with such scorn, such disdain, let alone if the said layman should have achieved a certain and quite respectable amount in his own particular field. However, as you may have gathered, I was first of all treated with a kind of reserve, then openly ridiculed. Consulting a veterinary scientist at the university, I fared little better. I wonder if any of them have since had a change of mind about the matter. On second thoughts, I wonder if any of them *could*
. . .

Just as it had been the telephone which had led to the discovery of an entire family having been the victims of these so far unexplained killers, it was also the telephone which led to the discovery of Wadjinup, an entire township — even if its population is (or *had* been, rather) only forty-odd people altogether — being attacked and left

31

without a single survivor. One of the victims hadn't even been a resident of the town, but merely a travelling salesman passing through on his way back to the city. God knows why he'd got out of his car, unless it had been to shoo off a flock of erstwhile harmless sheep from the road so that he could pass. But he *had* got out, and that had been the end of him.

I was not the only one to have my convictions; fortunately Beryl thought exactly the same. We needed to discuss the matter for only a few minutes before it occurred to both of us to verify from the Australian Yearbook that the population of Australia was in the vicinity of only thirteen million — people, that is — whereas the number of sheep estimated to be in the country was *two hundred* million. If, like a disease bacillus, the killer instinct had suddenly become contagious amongst them all, it would be roughly fifteen demented killers to every man, woman and child on the *island* continent. An *island* continent, mind you. No way out of it except by sea or air. And nothing much else in the way of land near it for a few thousand miles.

The eastern states, with more than 90 percent of the country's population, were safe enough, it seemed, with not only the desert but those extraordinary constructions, the rabbit-proof fences as well. But were these strong enough to confine sheep on the rampage? It didn't matter. The first report of a killing in New South Wales was soon followed by several, then countless more.

The Prime Minister made a special announcement to the nation, within just a few hours of Western Australia's State Premier asking him for urgent aid. The whole nation, including the island of Tasmania, was declared to be in a state of emergency.

It took only a few seconds after this announcement for me to make our flight reservations for overseas for as soon as possible. Even then, we still had three days to wait . . .

That night contact was lost with seventeen minor West Australian townships, two with a population over five hundred and one with over a thousand. Admittedly, all were confined in the one area, once a great sheep-rearing district — but that didn't make the horror any the less. Besides, the district was only just a little over a hundred miles from the capital city of Perth.

The following day, just as the army's few tank units and mobilized troops were being moved down to what had been designated a disaster area, all communication was lost with the considerable-sized town of Narrogin and its population of nearly five thousand. It was now estimated that up to ten thousand people had died, or inexplicably disappeared. It had become very much worse in the eastern states.

The army tanks were able to radio back that they had been brought to a halt just before the location where many miles of bush along the highway suddenly gave way to more open country and fields just before the small town of Williams. The convoy had been brought to a halt by, the field commander said, thousands of sheep blocking the way across the road and inexorably advancing through the tanks and trucks. Some of the convoy's vanguard had tried to turn around, but in the confusion (which was obviously an understatement for sheer panic) three tanks had become interlocked while a fourth was overturned on a steep embankment.

Shortly afterwards, the field commander was abruptly cut off and couldn't be contacted again. The army radio operator taking the report told *The Daily News*, the evening newspaper, that it had been difficult to hear any of what the field commander had been saying because of the incessant bleating of sheep. It had amounted, the radio operator had said, to almost a continual roar. He had never, he added, heard anything so terrifying in all his life.

That night all roads to the southwest portion of the state were cut off. Pinjarra, only 60 miles from the capital, and then the holiday resort town of Mandurah, went "dead", so to speak. News media reported that first hundreds and now thousands of panic-stricken refugees were streaming from the south into the city by the only two routes left open. Then the more inland of these was cut off and there was only the coast road left. The refugees were mostly in cars and trucks and commandeered buses, but some were on motorbikes and even bicycles. First arrivals in the metropolitan area said they didn't even dare think of what had happened to those who had been trying to escape on foot. And these first arrivals spoke with the same hysteria, the same gaping and frantic eyes, as they told of the onslaughts of sheep which had somehow suddenly acquired the appearance and terrifying characteristics of wolves. No one, now, dared make the old joke about sheep in wolves' clothing . . .

Then the radio and television news sessions reported that even the West Coast Road had been cut off. So far as the city knew, so were all roads from the north and east. There was no communication beyond a fifty-mile radius of the city. *Beyond* that radius, it was presumed, there were now only sheep.

I can only suppose that the government was doing all it could to avoid panic, but the urgency of the situation couldn't be concealed any longer, and the State Premier, James Riskin, made an announcement in a special broadcast over both television and radio to the effect that he had appealed to the country's Prime Minister not only for more troops but also for fighter bombers from the Air Force to kill the sheep by machine gun strafing, bombing or even chemicals.

The mention of chemicals led to an interview with Professor Sanders of the university, whose opinion was that the sheep had been suddenly struck by some kind of new virus which turned this normally docile animal into a ferocious carnivore, a common enough result obtained with laboratory experiments on guinea pigs, rats, dogs, monkeys and, yes, even sheep.

This was immediately followed by the national Minister for Foreign Affairs stating that it was now suspected that the virus was no accident but had been deliberately introduced by the Communists, though his department had not yet been able to verify as to whether the perpetrators of such an atrocity had been Russia or China. The implications of such a vile method in international warfare needed little further comment, he said, but he was confident that Australian scientists now working day and night on the problem would soon discover an antivirus which could be introduced, probably by spraying from the air, to prevent further spreading of the disease in the rest of the nation's sheep.

But it was only the following morning when Prime Minister Hawkins declared the entire nation to be in a state of emergency and that he had sought urgent help from both Britain and the United States. Meanwhile, the people were requested to keep calm, to remain in their homes with doors and windows securely closed and even locked, and, whenever it became necessary to venture outdoors only in vehicles which could be securely closed and locked against outside attack.

It was then announced with regret that, as had already happened with schools, all hospitals were now closed. From now on all victims would have to fend for themselves.

All ships and aircraft were fully booked. People made offers of fortunes to those with reservations, some of whom were even fool enough to take them. But then ships which were expected were suddenly diverted from Fremantle. Albany and Geraldton, of course, had been long out of the question. People waited, now, at the airport, taking what provisions they thought they might need while they waited, and of course all their portable valuables. Deeds for property and real estate, however, were already considered of no value whatsoever.

And this was how Beryl and I found the airport when we arrived there to catch our plane — at long last. We'd both got to the stage where we thought we wouldn't make it, before either the planes were cancelled for flights to Perth — or anywhere in Western Australia for that matter — or else the sheep would come down like wolves from the all too near hills.

We left the car where we could, as most others had done. I didn't even bother to take the keys out of the lock. As it was, we still had quite a walk, hurrying as fast as we could — and always, always, looking around us. Cars had been left abandoned as far back as the main highway flanking the airport, about a mile back. It was almost impossible trying to push our way through the crowd before the airport buildings. Armed police were everywhere, admitting only those with tickets for that evening's flights. But before getting through the police, you had to push your way through forests of desperately beseeching hands clutching notes and jewellery in quivering fingers, offering any sum you wanted to name for your plane tickets. Some, I saw, and tried to keep Beryl from seeing it, had had to be subdued by the police using their truncheons. There was a woman lying with her skull cracked open like an eggshell, her hand still clutching a sheaf of banknotes. No one bothered about them, *or* her, nor others who soon suffered the same fate. At least, I reflected, it was quick.

And yet I don't think this was the most horrible sight that was to confront us. There was almost as much bedlam inside the airport buildings as out. One of the worst things I was to see was a small girl clutching a doll to her as she swayed from side to side, singing to it:

Little Bo-Peep has lost her sheep
And doesn't know where to find them.
Leave them a—

But the child got no further. A man — it might not even have been her father — suddenly turned on her in fury, and before anyone could stop him, he had felled the child with just the one blow. I can only presume, and hope, that she died instantly. I hadn't been able to stop Beryl from seeing that one either, but we were both becoming pretty immune to it all by this time.

The plane did get away just after midnight, over three hours late. But it was lucky to get away at all. The sheep had come down from the hills towards the city and started streaming across the airport. We had to make a run for it.

Those trying to embark without having tickets to show at the steps were being shot and thrown bodily out of the way. Beryl and I only just made it; the steps were pulled away just after I'd been able to push us both in, the man behind us left frantic on the landing.

The people started to run for another plane warming up on the runway. Then some of them saw the sheep streaming towards them and started to run back towards the airport building. I didn't see any more. The door was slammed shut and the plane was already surging forward before we could even find our seats.

But seats hadn't been allocated. As it was, there were over a dozen more passengers than there were seats, and so we had to stand in the aisle — or try to. The plane lurched and bumped several times as it went down the runway, and I could only presume some of the sheep to have already been in its path. Yet we did manage to get off the ground, the last plane out of Western Australia.

I just got a glimpse of the other plane that was to have left immediately after us as we circled to gain height. It had tried to follow, but the sheep had balked its path. Through a window I saw it veer suddenly off the runway in its takeoff and just turn and tumble absurdly over, just like a child's toy. There was a little puff of light as it burst into flames; then it was cut off from view. Beryl had seen that, too; she was crying again. As had happened so often lately, I could feel her shaking and crying against me.

Eventually she said, "Is there any reason why it shouldn't be just the same at Adelaide? Or wherever we have to land next?"

"We don't go that way, thank God."

"We don't?"

"No. We go to Singapore."

"Don't — don't they have sheep there?"

"Not to my knowledge."

"And — and they can't swim?"

"Sheep? Not that far."

"Perhaps we should get off there, then. And stay there."

37

"We're not allowed. It's London or nowhere."

She was silent — just slumped against me, shaking again.

"What's the matter?" I asked her. "At least we've got *some* hope ahead of us — now. Not like all those other poor bastards we've left behind . . ."

But then, for once, she'd thought of something before I had.

She said, "They've got sheep in England, too, haven't they?"

At Singapore we weren't allowed out of the airport building, and even then not beyond the barrier leading to where Singaporeans and other transit passengers were allowed, and could be seen through the enormous windows. On the other side of those windows, rather like small and curious children, some of the local population — Chinese, Malays — pressed their faces, snubbing their noses, to look at us as though we were some kind of freaks. Then someone must have thought up what all of them were soon doing. It could have been meant as a joke, I suppose; but if it was, it was in pretty poor taste. Yet perhaps it had been triggered off merely by somebody jeering. Whatever it was, they were all suddenly opening their mouths wide and bleating at us.

"Baaaa! Baaaa! . . ."

When we turned away, it was only to be confronted by the television screens — with the last films flown out of Perth being shown on closed circuit expressly for our benefit. I suppose cameras with telephoto lenses had been used from the comparative safety of armoured tanks, or something like that. But it looked as though these terrifying animals were stampeding clean out of the screen to leap in amongst us all. Some of the women couldn't watch it; they either turned away or buried their faces in their hands. Some had started to moan. And some, of course, began to get hysterical again, especially at the scenes showing the sheep dragging people down and tearing and rending at them.

I remembered how I had once seen their mouths drool spittle from hunger and thirst; now they drooled blood.

And those little hoofs that kept on pounding and pounding . . .

Before we arrived in England, the rest of Australia was already gone — *and* New Zealand.

Beryl and I are now settled in London as I write this. We wouldn't dream of living in the country, of course. Reading this through, I can see how disjointed it all is and not at all in my usual style. But, quite understandably, it took me nearly three months to get over a nervous breakdown; in fact, I'm not at all sure that I'm over it yet.

But I must leave this now to get on to something else — a letter to the editor of *The Times*. For that piece in this morning's issue just can't be left like that, about the Somerset farmer being attacked and killed by wild dogs. They *weren't* wild dogs. I know.

Of course I am glad to have seen those press reports proclaiming that the holocaust in Western Australia has supposedly come to an end, and that the sheep are apparently quite docile again. I even believe that those television pictures transmitted by satellite showing the sheep grazing peacefully once more were possibly authentic and maybe not faked as they could so easily have been. No doubt the sheep *are* returned to normal — now that there are no human beings (or human animals?) left there to antagonize them. But what would happen, I wonder, if some of those observers who have flown at low altitudes over the country from the east of Australia to bring back those reports were to have their planes land and human figures step out to be seen by the sheep? Ah, that might be a very different tale — a very different tale indeed.

I realize that people won't listen to me. I even realize that they don't *want* to listen to me. After all, it's hardly a pretty prospect for them if they do. But surely at least *some* people must read those other newspaper reports, as small as they are, and nearly always tucked away in back pages?

Of all the Biblical prophecies, this is clearly the most horrible. But I suppose humanity does deserve it, and not only for what they've done to the humble sheep all through the ages — and more especially now — but more for what we've done to each other. We should have known, I suppose — for was there ever anything more meek to be the inheritors?

SPACEMAN

Lee Harding

I

Trapped between the sharp teeth of his trauma, Marnsworth remembered her smile. And other things. The way the rain fell on Hydria: soft and diffused and everywhere at once, as though some strange osmosis had sifted it through the pores of space — and colors so bright that his corroded mind ached with their memory.

The rain placed a warm film over everything it touched, softening every leaf and every garment on the island with a tireless patience quite unlike the other driving rains he had known; and the trembling colours imprisoned in his head had illuminated a part of himself that had always been deeply buried in the dark night of his soul.

It had been raining the last time they had stopped over on Island One. In fact, he couldn't recall a time when it had not been raining on that vast oceanic world and its scattered islands. Never once had he looked out over the island without the gentle pervading film of rain coming between himself and the landscape, while overhead an unseen sun burnished the deep layer of cloud a hazy shade of copper.

Hydria was only a whistlestop on the great bustle Outward. The water world was inexhaustible and it allowed the thirsty ships from Earth to drink their fill of reaction mass before they moved on with their urgent business of remaking the universe. There were richer prizes to be won than this almost landless world and the Service had contented itself with carving out a landfall and stop-over port for its ships on one of the equatorial islands. So perfunctory was this activity that they hardly bothered to give the place a name, only a number. Hydria had nothing more that they could plunder and so she was spared the indignities commensurate with terraforming, a rapacious process that had already moulded many brave new worlds in the delightful image of mother Earth.

Yes, it had been raining and the *Barain* had loomed large on the wet tarmac — a great metal canister from Earth, tended by Servicemen in their smooth plastic suits, moving around the base of the monolith like pale white grubs groping around the carcass of some dead animal.

Suiting up had become something of a ritual.

Marnsworth had first disposed of his captain's uniform and then pulled on a flimsy transparent plastic sheath over his underwear. It would insulate his body and ensure that it was maintained at the proper temperature regardless of his external environment. Over this he donned a heavier but in no way cumbersome survival suit. It was fitted out with a number of tiny powerpacks, from which fine cables sprouted like delicate vines, fed the thermostatic insulator underneath and provided power for the faint but adequate deadfield that radiated outward from the wide belt at his waist. He checked this carefully before he zipped shut the transparent parka fitted to the suit — the field would annihilate any dangerous micro-organisms for quite some distance around him, ensuring that he could venture safely beyond the controlled environment of his ship without fear of any serious contamination.

Such caution was necessary. Many lives had been forfeited in the early and clumsy days of space exploration to inadequate personnel protection. These days full survival suiting was mandatory for all Servicemen, even if they only stepped outside for a few moments to urinate.

More than a century of modifications had made living in spacesuits comfortable and he was the animal spirit of his age — a spaceman. A starship was his natural environment.

The *Barain* surrendered him to the Island. He was escalated to ground level with all the care that a child could expect from its mother. He planted his protected feet on the wet tarmac and waited while they broke out a skiff.

He looked up and felt a sudden longing for the clear controlled skies of Earth. Through the sifting rain he could barely distinguish the Service buildings crowding the perimeter of the field. Fine detail was blurred by the pervading drizzle, so that they loomed squat and ugly in the coppery sunlight. Vaguely he could discern the figures of some local landmen lounging against the buildings and studying the stranded starship. They seemed not to notice the rain, seemed also to draw some nourishment from the humid wetness and the pallid sunshine. Their chests were bared to both and they were probably prepared to spend the rest of their lives covered with the same warm film of moisture that was clouding his parka. If their dull faces had anything to communicate it was obliterated by the drifting rain.

High up in the belly of the *Barain* a panel opened and a compact surface craft nosed its way out. A driver adept at his task guided the skiff down to a neat landing only a few paces away from where Damian Marnsworth waited. The captain stepped forward impatiently, thanked the young Serviceman and assumed solitary command of the sleek craft.

He sat down before the sparsely detailed instrument panel, fidgeted nervously with the toggles and switches. It had been some time since he had driven a surface craft and, although it was capable of automatic piloting, he felt it essential that he become confident with the few manual controls before he moved off.

He looked straight ahead, trying to pierce the solid veil of water that enveloped the hazy outlines of the landfall buildings. Beyond them stretched the great rain forests of Island One that had swallowed up Gerard Childers and now kept him jealously hidden from the *Barain* and its crew.

Childers had been the best drivesman he had ever known. He had disappeared several stopovers ago. An immediate, quick and cursory search of the settlement had been sufficient to convince Marnsworth that his man had taken to the forest and was too well hidden for them to be able to flush him out with the limited time at their disposal.

Childers had timed his break for the very last few minutes of landfall time. Once the initial flurry of excitement had been over Marnsworth had had no recourse but to up-ship on schedule and return to Earth with his second drivesman in charge of the engines.

Technicians were plentiful and Service Schedules were, like all parts of the Plan, impressively expensive. Each day spent away from Earth cost the administration mega-credits and the eager expansion of Earth's embryonic stellar empire was being accomplished with all the thoroughness that three centuries of red tape could muster. A maximum of eight hours stopover was mandatory for all ships and any captain who exceeded this limit without proper justification was quickly broken.

A minor technician just wasn't worth it.

But for Damian Marnsworth the situation went deeper than that; so deep that it hurt and had left a small weeping wound that refused to heal. Gerard Childers had been more than a mere technical subordinate — he had been a friend. They had schooled together and stepped out in the great ships to master space together and in this respect Childers' desertion had assumed the quality of a moral betrayal. He had left without a word of explanation, without any warning whatsoever — but this day Marnsworth was determined to challenge the rain forests and wrest from Childers the reason for his madness.

In his hands he held a map, a clumsy effort drawn by one of the local landmen the trip before last. It had cost him a considerable amount of money — but not so much that it could not be safely written off into petty cash — and the information he had drawn from it and fed into the skiff's auto-pilot would guide him to Childers. Marnsworth had wormed the crude drawing out of a drunken recluse in the Service bar — perhaps it was the way landmen disintegrated their society and fragmented into so many different forms that made them seem so disgusting — and he had been restlessly waiting for an opportunity that would enable him to put it to use.

And this time he had one. Deep in the *Barain*'s belly an overstressed and underserviced main drive unit was undergoing urgently needed repairs. The work would take several days. The task was complex and only when the chief engineer had the massive engine stripped down and examined would he know what to do and how long it would take to reassemble and test the unit.

There would be plenty of time. The clear canopy of the skiff was already beaded with moisture. Marnsworth moved a toggle that set the auto-pilot in motion. The skiff moved skyward, hesitated for a moment several hundred feet above the tarmac while it checked the coordinates for Childers' hideout and then skimmed off over the settlement in the direction of the great northern rain forest.

As he passed over the shallow line of buildings Marnsworth saw several faces turned up toward the skiff. They were local landmen and for a brief moment he could see them clearly enough to note the wet hair plastered against their faces — he looked quickly away. All Servicemen shared this instinctive aversion to landmen, if only because they were living proof that the Plan was not always infallible. Genetic prediction and selection were still infant sciences — but time would improve the techniques of control so that deviations from the goal would become fewer and ultimately disappear, and the Empire would be populated by a truly space-bred society. In the meantime the Administration maintained a tolerant attitude toward its outcasts and sometimes even supported them in their absurd little enterprises. The unwanted world had become an ideal dumping place for social misfits.

The settlement disappeared behind him. The clouds and the rain closed in. The skiff gradually sought altitude so that it would be prepared for the mountain range that began some distance ahead.

II

Island One was shaped like a blunt heart, inclined southeast across the equator. At the southern, narrower end were two smaller islands grouped a few miles apart about thirty miles offshore, inhospitable rocks unworthy even of the numbers doled out to their larger brothers by the original cartographers of Hydria.

The island was heavily timbered and bore a crooked back underneath the lush, wet forests. This serrated ridge crossed the island from east to west and was the closest thing to a mountain range that the fresh young world had ever known. It made a long, slow climb for the small surface craft.

But Marnsworth was in no particular hurry now that the journey had finally been instigated. He had spent most of his life on board some sort of spacecraft, studying interminable viewscreens and printouts and had managed to achieve a most sought-after function of all Servicemen — he could almost switch himself off for long periods of time and allay the boredom of travel. And he did so now. He relaxed and waited, for this was the measure of his trade.

More out of idleness than from any genuine curiosity, he activated the external sensors of the skiff. The whispered sounds of the world below drifted into the cabin. But the forest did not chatter incessantly like some forests he had known; nor did it scream or whimper. No predator moved through the unseen undergrowth. Here dominion had been divided between birds and insects and an occasional herbivore and that explained why the ecology of the island had always moved at such an infinitesimal rate — time had barely touched this great world of water.

He drowsed. Perhaps he should have felt nervous and excited at the prospect of tracking down Gerard Childers but emotions that could overpower his logical mind had been bred from his strain several generations ago. He almost slept until the skiff broke through the clouds and challenged the timberline. A bare sky gaped momentarily before him and a golden sun burned bright and naked into his face. He looked away.

The land that swept back from the narrow ridge of mountains reminded him of the great game reserves of Africa. The broad veldt-like stretches were a striking contrast to the rain-drenched landscape he had been travelling over.

The skiff soared easily over the flimsy backbone of the island and plunged straight down into a dense mist. The wound in the sky healed over and the clouds closed in. He relaxed again in his seat and checked his watch against the tripmeter on the control panel.

Ninety-seven minutes and one hundred and eleven miles away from the settlement. The long climb had slowed down the skiff but now that the mountains had been passed it was downhill all the way to Childers' retreat.

He had rehearsed all sorts of dialogues with himself but now that he was close to his quarry he found that he could cast serious doubts on them all. What would he say? What could he say? At the moment he could think of nothing that wouldn't sound offensive and presumptuous. Perhaps — and this was what he wished — perhaps they would both blunder their way through the initial confrontation and then, over a pleasant drink or two, some of the friendship they had shared might begin to flow between them again.

He missed that more than anything else. Space had become withdrawn and lonely since Childers had deserted the Service. There had been a time when the universe had been their oyster. Whatever had possessed Childers to turn his back to it in such a perfunctory manner?

Without any warning the mist and rain disappeared. The skiff plunged into a wide valley. Gone were the rain forests and the sparse veldts, to be replaced by sweeping grasslands. A river broke free from the distant forest and played tag under the speeding craft. The land began to rise steeply on either side and finally pushed it, roaring and foaming whitely, through a narrow gorge and out into another, narrower valley. The skiff shot quickly through this natural pass and, once it had entered the valley beyond, began to describe a wide gliding arc that broke for the first time the singleminded purpose of its flight.

A persistent beeping began on the control panel.

Marnsworth tensed. A human habitation lay somewhere ahead. Childers' retreat — or somebody else's? Was the map a fake?

He had thought of radioing ahead to announce his arrival but he wasn't sure that Childers would appreciate a call. There was no point in putting his old friend unnecessarily on edge.

Cultivated fields passed by underneath. He leaned forward, the better to observe the new landscape. Human hands had moulded this land to some purpose. Neat plantations of some sort of bush spread down the river's edge. This was no fetid swamp — Childers had chosen well. Perhaps his madness was not quite as intense as Marnsworth had imagined — this landscape had been designed with great care and affection.

The skiff accelerated briefly to grab an extra few feet of altitude to fly over a wide belt of trees. It dropped abruptly into an enormous clearing. A small white house, festooned with colourful creepers, was set almost in the very centre of this smooth area. It was U-shaped, its front aspect facing southwest so that it took in the curving elbow of the river, the dim mountains in the distance — hidden now by tumbling rain clouds — and Marnsworth's descending surface craft.

The control panel beeped three times and was still. The skiff hovered expectantly, waiting for Marnsworth to resume manual control and descend. But a cold nervousness had suddenly gripped him. It made him fumble at the controls with fingers that had suddenly become inexpert. He wondered if the common audacity of his visit had been ill-planned. What sort of a reception could he expect from a man who was already three years a stranger?

Well, he would soon find out. No sense turning back now that he had come this far.

He sent the skiff gliding cautiously down. It settled on the grass and he cut the motors and sat for a few breathless moments while they idled away into silence. There was such an unnatural calm about the valley that he was reluctant to disfigure the silence with any abrupt movement.

There was no sign of activity from the house, no indication that his arrival had been noted. Either Childers did not possess even a rudimentary sensor or he was deaf — or disinterested.

Marnsworth slipped out of his seatbelt and swung back the canopy. He jumped lightly to the ground. His suit lacked an amplifier, but the light gravity of Hydria made movement effortless even for his meagre muscles. He felt the wet grass give under his weight. The outside temperature was high — so was the humidity — but his suit filtered out these unpleasant environmental things. He flicked on his sensors and allowed the moist and quiet sounds of Island One to make an impression.

He was still standing in the same spot several minutes later when the front door of the white house swung open. He saw a figure hesitating behind the deep shadow. Then it stepped forward into the sunlight.

Marnsworth gave a start. At first he wasn't sure that this actually was Gerard Childers but as the man moved toward him with bold, unfrightened steps, he realised with a sinking heart that this — this creature — was indeed his old friend but scarcely recognizable, with the upper half of his body bared to the weather and with a heavy growth of beard disfiguring his face. He wore only a pair of dun shorts and his bare feet crushed the wet grass.

The sensors in Marnsworth's suit were sensitive. They picked up the words the other man was mumbling.

"Damian — good God, what brings you here?"

The outward appearance of his friend might have been transfigured by life under such alien conditions but at least the voice was familiar. Marnsworth stepped forward eagerly, reached out and Childers gripped his plastic hand and pumped it vigorously.

"Hello, Gerard." He felt shy and foolish, as though he didn't really belong here, so far from his ship. "I came out to see what you've been doing with yourself."

Childers smile held an uncomfortable edge. "I hope you haven't come to try and impress me back into the Service or anything like that?"

Marnsworth shook his head. "No. It's just that — well, the ship's laid up for a few days at the settlement. I thought I'd take advantage of the break to come and look you up, find out what you've been doing these past few years."

Childers seemed to relax a little.

"Always knew that rustbucket would let you down one day."

"Oh, it's not the *Queen*," Marnsworth explained. "The *Barain*. A new ship. This is only her third trip out. Her main drive's been giving us hell ever since she was commissioned —"

Childers placed a brawny, suntanned arm around Marnsworth's plastic shoulders and guided him toward the house.

"Well, it isn't every day we get a visiting spaceman —"

The house was cool inside but Marnsworth could detect no threshold whirr of conditioning, so he did not unzip his parka.

Childers eyed him quizzically.

"Aren't you going to take that damned thing off?"

Without waiting for an answer he moved across the room and slid back a panel in the wall to reveal an array of bottles and glasses. Marnsworth began to feel welcome but a residue of his curious embarrassment remained. He gestured awkwardly with his smooth hands.

"I hope you realize that you've had a damned sight longer to get used to this air than I have."

Childers looked up from the dark drink he was pouring.

"Oh, yes. I'd forgotten that. Does that mean you'd turn your nose up at a local beverage?"

"Hardly likely."

"Good."

Marnsworth took a deep breath and unzipped his parka. He shivered as the humid air struck his face and his hand shook a little when it reached for the drink.

The beverage was raw and unfamiliar and it fought its way down his throat like a living animal. But once it had arrived in his belly he found he could experience an agreeable warmth spreading through his body — intoxicants could vary in taste but their effect never varied from one world to another. He found the stuffiness in the air most disagreeable but at this stage he felt much too polite to create any difficulties.

Childers motioned him into a chair and sat down beside him.

"Don't often have people up from the settlement," he said. "At least, not Service people."

Marnsworth found his chair uncomfortable. It had been hewn from some natural material and was quite hard beneath him. But he made no comment and avoided looking directly at Childers. He still felt residual horror at the changes in his friend. Something other than the fierce u.v. had burned Childers' face into hard, coarse lines and bleached his hair with wide bands of gray.

Both men were in their middle forties but in contrast to his host Marnsworth had the bland, untroubled and smooth face of an adolescent. He sat behind his suit and it nursed him and cared for him, in much the same manner as his ship looked after him while they moved between one world and another, one year and the next. He was slim and fragile and unaccustomed to the hardships of living on the land. His environment was space and his strength could be found a hundred thousandfold in any of the amplifiers he was called upon to use.

Was it possible that Childers had been unable to maintain his rejuvenants since he had left the Service? Was that why he looked so old after only three short years?

Marnsworth coughed discreetly, suggesting that the liquor had troubled his throat.

"You seem to have settled in rather well."

One had to be sociable, otherwise an embarrassed silence would engulf them.

Childers managed a wry grimace. "Well, the first few months were the worst. After that, well, everything became a little easier."

"I see." But no, he did not really see. "The — acclimatization?"

"Something like that. You like the wine?"

Marnsworth said that he did — with reservations — and accepted another.

The house was large by the standards he was accustomed to. Plenty of wide, full-length windows to let in the coppery sunlight and if the furniture seemed sparse and crude by some standards, it was at least functional. It was the excess of free space that he found most disconcerting. On board ship and at home — in fact anywhere on Earth, for that matter — living space was at a premium. Marnsworth had been tailored to fit a cramped environment — and to fit graciously, without asking awkward questions.

Childers was staring down at his drink. Without looking up he said, "I suppose you'd like to know why I left?"

Marnsworth did not answer but let him continue.

"Well, it was just something I had to do, that's all. Then and there — at that moment. Without any temporizing. But I'm sorry if you've been through any trouble."

No, no trouble, Marnsworth thought. *Only pain.*

"But you see, there wasn't time to — to think about things like that. About the Service. About command and all those other meaningless things. I just couldn't stand being locked up inside that great tin can any longer. I had to get out."

"And so you threw up your work, your career, your pension," Marnsworth said. "And for what, Gerard, for what?" He gestured to take in their surroundings. "For this?"

Childers didn't answer. And his face had not yet lifted from contemplating an empty glass.

Marnsworth felt failure like a great weight lodged in his lungs.

"All I know, Gerard, is that you've changed — changed much since I saw you last. And have you done it all for this?"

Childers raised his head slowly and there was an honesty in his eyes that had not been there before.

"You haven't changed much at all," he said and then looked quickly away, as though embarrassed by what he saw. "As you've probably guessed, I haven't been taking my shots since I left the Service — and there's a rather frightening change in the first six months or so. But after that things tend to even out and you get used to your new appearance. You put on weight. If you're working, then you start building muscles. The sun tans you — your body sweats. A lot of things happen. But I guess it's in the face that a man shows it most."

Suddenly furious, Marnsworth jumped to his feet. "I can understand anybody wanting out," he cried, "but why in God's name did you throw away your youth?"

Childers looked puzzled. "But did I do that, Damian? Did I really? Has it ever occurred to you just how costly those treatments are when you haven't access to Service wages? Not everyone back home can afford them either — or perhaps you've conveniently forgotten that? Spacemen tend to forget everything that is not absolutely necessary to their profession. And I found that I could do without my shots — as I could do without most of the things that Earth had given me. Once you have discarded one myth you can discard them all."

Marnsworth said nothing and Childers continued.

"Did you know that rejuvenation is our greatest lie? Oh, we keep ourselves young on the surface, on the skin where it shows — at least those of us who can afford to do so — but it's only a sickly veneer. The flesh may stay young but our minds aren't fooled. They're much too clever to be tricked by our smart little drugs. We age our mind through experience, regardless of the physical rejuvenation that continually remakes us — but what, do you suppose, will be the end of all this? Will our minds get surfeited with accumulated inertia and finally stop from sheer exhaustion? I suppose it would be interesting to find out — but I no longer wish for that sort of knowledge. I have — other things."

Marnsworth was breathing heavily in the humid atmosphere. His eyes were bright. "Some day," he said, "some day they will find a way to —"

"To rejuvenate the mind? How awful. But I suppose they will do it if they've set their minds to it. Man has made a habit of accomplishment. But really — one doesn't need their clever chemicals. Rejuvenation of a tired mind is a simple process for those who are prepared to look. I found it here. Others look elsewhere."

Marnsworth realized that he was as far from Gerard Childers as he had been back at the settlement. Was there no way of bridging this enormous gulf?

"Gerard," he began, his voice soft and patient, "do you remember how we used to talk in the old days, back at school?"

"About how big the universe was and how mankind would chart its secrets and what an adventure it would be —"

"To be part of it —"

"And wouldn't it be grand?"

"Then you haven't forgotten?"

"No, of course not. But that was all so long ago, Damian, and we were such fools."

"But your training — all those years —"

"And for what? A few years out of my life — not worth crying over. Oh, I won't deny that I was once as starry-eyed as any young cadet —"

"You were more than that. You were one of the foremost physicists of your time — and the best damned drivesman I ever knew. And you left it all — ran away like some crazy kid. And only for this!"

A shadow passed across Childers' face. He became very serious.

"Listen, Damian. I will tell you something. Something very important to me — and to everybody. When I had finished all those wonderful years of schooling, of breaking God down into little pieces so that I could measure Him and analyze Him and wondering what to do with what I found — after I had accumulated all this useless knowledge, do you know where I found myself? That's right — staring at gauges and meters and tapping out commands to machines more clever than myself, nursing spaceships through hyper-space and watching little coloured lights winking on and off. And that was all, Damian — only that. Ten years of my life studying so that I would wind up acting as caretaker to a machine."

"But such work demands that sort of study," Marnsworth protested. "Surely you don't expect —"

"I expect nothing — not any more. Only never to waste my life in such a useless fashion. I want to feel the pressure of a world beneath my feet; I want fresh air in my lungs and not the canned stuff we're too used to accepting as the real thing. I don't want to have to drag my environment around with me to every God-forsaken corner of the universe. Damn it all, we've become a race of galactic sculptors running around the cosmos putting Earth's face on every habitable world we find — can't you see that's blasphemous?"

III

Marnsworth's thoughts were locked in a nexus of consternation; he could not speak. Impatient words had piled up into an unmanageable lump in his throat and his lips twitched in an agitation to free them. His whole body was shaking inside the protective suit.

The fierce light faded suddenly from Childers' eyes. He looked past Marnsworth and his face softened. The spaceman followed the direction of his gaze and was surprised to find a young woman standing in the doorway.

Childers stood up. "Rachel, this is Damian Marnsworth — Captain Marnsworth. My old chief. Damian — my wife."

Her quiet entry helped to break the terrible stasis that had gripped the spaceman. He struggled awkwardly to his feet and dipped his head sharply in a gentleman's acknowledgment.

"What a pleasant surprise, Mrs. Childers," he said. "I had no idea —"

He had assumed that Childers lived alone in his retreat — nobody had mentioned the woman. She was extraordinarily attractive even to a spaceman's eyes — but she was regarding him with a cold grace he found disquieting.

She wore a simple orange shift and her dark body — darker even than her husband's — moved visibly underneath the material as she crossed the room. Probably quite a bit of African and Eurasian somewhere along the line, he reckoned — particularly when one considered the almost imperceptible slant of her luminous dark eyes. Her body was strong, supple and well proportioned, if slightly plump by some standards and her jet-black hair was pulled back into a bun at the base of her neck. She extended a courteous hand to Marnsworth but she did not succeed in concealing the hostility in her eyes.

"How very nice to see you, Captain." Her voice was soft and husky. It disturbed Marnsworth. "You are — most welcome. We don't often have people from the Service visiting us."

He grasped her moist hand with his plastic fingers and sensed her displeasure like a mild electric shock passing up his arm.

"Thank you."

Childers made a disparaging noise.

"Damn fool lives in that suit. You'll never get him out of it, that's for sure."

Feeling a trifle foolish, Marnsworth explained to the woman — in detail — why his survival suit was necessary and how unaccustomed he was to being off-ship. While he talked her ambivalence seemed to soften a little.

"You have a very nice — ah — estate here," he babbled on, unable to stop now for fear that the terrible nexus would grab him again. "Mrs. Childers, I must confess that I never —"

"Oh, for God's sake, call her Rachel, will you?" Childers exploded, exasperated. And then turned attentively to his wife. "Would you like a drink?"

She nodded. While her husband poured one for her she moved gracefully across the room and sat down on an upholstered divan under the east window. The copper sunlight made her skin blaze. The vivid color of the shift was almost blinding to Marnsworth's weak, spaceman's eyes. She crossed her legs and Marnsworth realized that her feet were bare, like her husband's.

Of course she had timed her entry with discretion, waiting until the two old friends had established some sort of rapport and then, with the penchant for perfect timing that only beautiful women seemed to possess, had announced herself when her presence was most needed — her arrival had made their disagreements unimportant for the moment.

"When do you have to be back?" Childers asked.

"Well, I don't really know. That damned drive could take days to fix and —"

"Then why not stay here with us for a while? Have yourself a holiday away from that damned Service —" He bit his lip and shrugged apologetically, realizing he had made a mistake. "Matter of fact, Rachel and I are visiting some friends of ours this evening — a sort of party, you might call it. I think you'd enjoy yourself. As I remember, you were always one for a good time."

A good time . . .

The words had meant something once, long ago, between schooling and the Service, when there had been time for things without Purpose. Something else that Marnsworth had forgotten.

They were both watching him — the woman sipping at her wine, frankly curious, Childers with an edge of nervousness about him he seemed not quite able to understand. Marnsworth sniffed. It was a painful gesture — his sinuses were swollen and irritated and he was finding it difficult to breathe.

"You see," Childers elaborated, "there's quite a colony of us around here. Murray's place is only about fourteen miles north, on the other side of the river. Every month we had a get-together at each other's place — we take turns — and generally have ourselves a ball. It's only when you're isolated from people for a great deal of time that you begin to appreciate their company. I know you're probably anxious to get back to your ship but we'd be delighted to have you with us, wouldn't we Rachel?"

Marnsworth looked at the woman. Only her eyes were visible as she raised her glass to her lips. She inclined her head a little to one side and her answer was a husky whisper.

"Of course."

Marnsworth fidgeted nervously. "Well —" What could he say? Of course he felt uncomfortable but an insatiable curiosity made him want to find out more about these people. There was an enigma here he should be able to understand. "If you think it would be all right with your friends?"

Childers laughed and looked relieved. "But of course they won't mind. And wait until you see what a fine bunch of people we've got here."

Childers placed a brawny arm around Marnsworth's narrow shoulders and grabbed his arm excitedly. On the divan the woman sipped her drink and studied Marnsworth thoughtfully with a distant and impenetrable expression.

Dusk came slowly to the island. No spectacular sunset transfigured the dull sky — the coppery haze simply faded gradually away, as though a finely adjustable rheostat had been brought into play.

Marnsworth had spent most of the afternoon wandering around Childers' estate in the company of his old friend. In the process he had come to understand the activities that occupied the ex-Serviceman but he was still no nearer to comprehending his motives.

Childers tilled and cultivated many acres by hand and the use of a few simple tools — there were no automatons that Marnsworth could see. The main crop was coffee, a local transplanting that had thrived at this altitude and enabled Childers and his wife to live comfortably. Export of the popular beans ensured that the space people and their home world could enjoy the occasional draught of a non-synthetic stimulant, although the price levied on outworld goods was prohibitively high for all but the chosen elite.

"I understand it retails back home for something like five credits an ounce," Childers observed, "and that's refined and adulterated."

"Five thirty-four," Marnsworth corrected.

"Is that so?" Childers smiled ruefully. "Well, Service pays us five and a half cents a pound — I can't imagine that all that extra is made up of freight and handling. Somebody has sure cornered themselves a market in natural coffee."

"You don't seem concerned that somebody is making an enormous profit from all your work."

"Huh? Oh, I can't be bothered about those things, Damian. They can do what they like after it leaves my hands. Everything I care for is here. They can have the rest."

The rain had persisted all afternoon. Now they sat in comfortable cane chairs on the veranda of Childers' house and watched the sunlight fade from the heavy clouds. Marnsworth had apologized and zipped up his parka several hours earlier. He had been unable to tolerate the

59

oppressive island atmosphere any longer. The constant fall of fine rain and the high humidity were causing pain through his nasal cavities and putting a constricting sensation into his chest where the unfiltered air rampaged. Now the subtle mechanisms whirred soundlessly in his suit and flushed out the excessive moisture and warmth, so that his breathing became easier and a little of the discomfort was eased out of his head.

He sat and stared at the soft curtain of moisture. Occasionally a light breeze would puff some of it toward the house and it would fall like sea-spray upon the verandah.

"Does it ever stop?" he asked.

"Sometimes. Do you find it depressing? We don't really notice it any more — not when it falls like this. One of the many advantages of having a low surface gravity. Point six-eight — or is it six-four? I seem to have forgotten."

Childers' eyes were bright and clear and he could see well out into the darkening landscape. But Marnsworth's view had been obscured for some time by the distorting film of moisture on the outside of his parka.

"Is this why you left the Service? Simply to be a landman? To move dirt around with your fingers and never know the stars again?"

Childers looked up at the dark clouds where the stars were rarely visible.

"If you mean, did I come here only for that, then I can't really answer you. You see, we've only begun to discover what we want to do. I've been too busy relearning what it is to be myself to worry about motivations — but yes, I like it here. We like it here. I can't think of going back to the Service — even if they would have me, which I doubt — so where's the sense of asking?"

"Because I have to know."

"Why, Damian? Why is it important that you should know why I came here when I don't even know the multileveled answer myself? All I know is that I could never be a Serviceman again — not with all that emptiness outside crowding to get in. I guess I just wasn't made for it. Maybe Control goofed. It must happen sometimes.

Sure, they mould us into a pattern, but how much can they motivate our subconscious? I believe that there are worlds — and Hydria is one of them — that reach out to some deep part of us we are unaware of and these worlds communicate with our subconscious in a way that Control never planned. But only some of us have need of and heed their summons. The misfits. The failures. The dropouts. The ones ill-wrought by Control." He laughed and waved a hand at Marnsworth's distorted and horrified face behind the clouded parka. "Oh, don't worry, Damian — you're all right, I think. Control made a fine job of you. But with me — and some others — they were clumsy. You are a creature of space — something new. But Rachel and I are landpeople. Perhaps the ultimate destiny of the human race is to put a fresh new face on the universe — one day they might even find some way of fitting out Earth with some fantastic sort of drive that will enable them to take their whole synthetic world out to the stars. But our roots are deeper, Damian. We love the land. There is something there that spaceman should not entirely forget."

"But your youth —" Marnsworth struggled to speak. "Why did you discard your youth?"

Childers shrugged and smiled an enigmatic smile. "It's late," he said, getting up and studying the encroaching darkness. "We'd best go inside and get ready or we'll have Rachel on our backs."

Numerous exits led off the main room but Marnsworth could see no doors.

An open house — how very extraordinary . . .

Rachel was waiting for them. She was standing at one of the exits — or entrances — a slight impatience in her manner. She had changed into a plain white smock that came freely down to mid-thigh and exposed her long brown limbs to advantage. She was barefoot still — it seemed to be a custom of the island — and her dark skin made a dramatic contrast with the smock. As he moved closer Marnsworth saw that she had some arrangement in her hair — he realized with surprise that it was a fresh red

61

flower. He saw beads of moisture still on it.

A peculiar people . . .

He felt suddenly ill at ease. He had opened his parka again from a desire to be courteous to this woman but suddenly, facing her like this, ready to leave, he felt a little conspicuous in his survival suit. He wondered if it had been such a good idea to agree to attend the local festivity or whatever it was called.

Childers deciphered his indecision.

"Don't worry about that," he said quickly, indicating Marnsworth's suit. "They won't mind — really they won't."

And am I to be a specimen — a curiosity? Marnsworth's confidence had been badly shaken in the past few hours. Could he, just this once, and for only a few hours, submit to some small discomfiture, so that he might meet these people as an equal and not some oddity from Earth?

"If you have something I can wear," he said, "I'll leave this stuff behind. I'd feel a bit of a fool, you know, walking in on your friends like this."

Rachel smiled and he found a new warmth in her eyes.

"But of course," she said and turned back through the entrance. "I'll get you something."

A few minutes later she returned and handed the spaceman a pair of tan shorts and a bone-coloured sleeveless jacket from her husband's wardrobe. The jacket was a trifle big but the shorts, he saw with relief, were a stretch fabric. He took them and then stood feeling foolish while they stared at him.

It was a bad moment. And then Rachel, with an intuitive understanding of the situation, whisked back out of the room murmuring something about makeup.

Marnsworth hastily stripped off his suit — he stood naked for a moment like a skinned vegetable.

"It must feel strange," Childers observed, "after all this time."

Which was true enough. A spaceman was not accustomed under social conditions or aboard ship to exposing overmuch of himself. Not even back home, where one always swam in carefully filtered waters and alone and . . .

He dressed as quickly as he could in the strange outfit the woman had provided.

The solitary wan moon of Hydria was struggling to pierce the clouds when they left the house — only a pale glow was visible on the horizon. They left — not in Marnsworth's skiff but in a similar machine adapted to Childers' requirements. It was low and wide with ample cargo space in the rear and a single bench seat up front. They sat close together and Marnsworth was uncomfortably conscious of the nearness of Childers' wife, of her pressing against him and of the rich, musky odour of her skin. The subtle perfume she had sprinkled over her body did not completely mask this unpleasantness from his suddenly critical olfactory sensibilities. But it didn't offend him as much as it should. Something — perhaps the very strangeness of the environment he was experiencing so directly — had induced in his thoughts a delightful euphoria, so he relaxed and let his mind wander, instead of marshalling it disagreeably for the evening ahead.

The sky cleared in patches where some small stars sputtered. Something gripped his stomach and he looked quickly away. Outside the perpetual drizzle enveloped the clear canopy of the craft.

The journey could not have taken more than twenty minutes but for Marnsworth it was a time of increasing discomfort. He was unaccustomed to this sort of proximity, sandwiched between two people as lightly clad as himself. And the air inside the skiff had become increasingly sticky. The odour of his own sweat mingled with that of Childers and his wife. He could feel it running down his sides in small, embarrassing rivulets. His naked arms were slick with moisture and he could feel Rachel's warm wet shoulder pressing against his own — nervous sidelong glances showed him that her white shift had darkened in patches where it stretched tightly across her breasts. Once he shifted uneasily and she turned and smiled, considerately, as though she were aware of his discomfort and were trying to reassure him that the flight would soon be over.

His head did not feel too bad. With the lowering of the sun the temperature had dropped considerably and this made the general humidity easier to bear.

A white arc of the river blazed suddenly before them in the newly victorious moonlight. The skiff dropped toward a cluster of bright lights along one shore.

"That's it," Childers announced.

Marnsworth breathed a cautious sigh of relief.

A large clearing was spread out below them. From this height the surrounding forest glittered through the drizzle like a miniature fairyland.

"Murray's wife loves decor," Rachel explained. "She just adores lighting the place up for these get-togethers."

They landed near a group of similar machines at the edge of the clearing. Childers swung back the canopy and climbed out, motioning to Marnsworth to follow.

The spaceman tensed, then dropped lightly to the ground. His body reacted predictably at the feel of wet grass underneath his bare feet but he did what he could to dispel the revulsion. He turned around and extended his hand automatically to Childers' wife. She accepted it, a glimmer of old-world charm in her eyes, and climbed down from the skiff. Her hand was soft, moist and warm, like his own.

"Thank you," she said.

They looked at each other for a fragment of time and Marnsworth could see that, although she had not managed to completely suppress a mixture of distaste and amusement, she had thawed gradually toward him. He still sensed a remaining difference between them — a region of acceptance beyond which she was not prepared to move. Perhaps it was the gulf that had always existed and was continually widening between landpeople and the space society Marnsworth was part of.

"This way," Childers directed and led them across the

lawn toward the gaily decorated patio. A number of people were already assembled. Marnsworth had the uneasy feeling that the group had been buzzing with conversation prior to their arrival and that a sudden silence had descended upon them when they had failed to recognize Childers' companion.

Childers introduced him around. They were all dressed more or less alike, in the casual manner of the island. The men were mostly bare-chested and in shorts — the women wore short, filmy dresses and sleeveless, bolero-type vests. Some were naked from the waist up, like their menfolk. But it was the colours of the clothes that surprised Marnsworth. These people seemed to prefer the loudness of primary colours the way some people wanted their music played always at a high, ear-crashing volume. In the dazzling illumination the vivid blues and reds and yellows seemed to possess a strange life of their own — he had never before seen a group so gaily and dramatically dressed. Each individual was wrapped in his own bright haze, trapped by the sifting rain and the constantly changing lights. Marnsworth blinked constantly under the assault and moved sometimes like a man only half awake.

Finally he was introduced to Murray Wiseman. The spacemen found him to be an anachronism of his age, a stout man. His belly protruded well over the top of his shorts and his navel was a monstrous exclamation. He had a great thick thatch of body hair that the rain had slicked down all over his chest but, with the exception of a few miserable gray tufts around his ears, he was quite bald. His pate shone wetly under the lights — the film of moisture had made it a fine reflective surface.

"So this is your visitor." He pumped Marnsworth's hand soundly. His eyes were alive and fierce and they made the spaceman want to turn away.

"Damian Marnsworth," Childers introduced. "He's from the Service — a captain. And my old boss. Got his ship laid up for a few days and popped out to see us. Damian, this is Murray Wiseman."

"Well, enjoy yourself, enjoy yourself," Murray

admonished. "We don't often have visitors from outside."

He nodded to Rachel and then moved off to join his other guests.

Marnsworth felt strange. His head began to swim and he reached out to take hold of a balustrade. He felt that he was drowning in an ocean of age. The faces of the guests moved around him like ragged leaves in a whirlpool — he had never seen so many old people. On each and every one of them death seemed to have made a claim and worked an insidious pleasure.

Rachel's fingers clamped around his arm where it clung to the balustrade.

"Come over here."

He allowed her to lead him away from the patio toward the darker area of the clearing. She found him a seat and told him to sit down. He smiled sheepishly. And he was glad that she was at least adequately dressed — he had been shocked to see that some of the women here had decided to wear only skirts or shorts. There were some things so repulsive about old age that one should avoid displaying them. Not that anybody here was much past forty. It was the ugly patina of aging in all their faces that he found disquieting.

"Stay here," she suggested, "and take it easy. I'll get you something to drink."

A few minutes later she reappeared with a small wooden tray loaded with dishes filled with fine food and two small mugs of red wine.

"Here, try some of this."

He sat up.

"I don't know if I should."

One had to be careful eating off-ship.

"Gerard chose the food," she explained. "He said it shouldn't interfere with your delicate digestion." Her smile was mischievous. "And the wine will help. It's very gentle."

He found that it was. His stomach did not complain, so he investigated some of the unfamiliar savouries Childers had piled up on the tray.

"Are you my guardian angel for the evening?" he asked.

His breath had become a little laboured and he wished he had brought along his suit, just in case.

She laughed.

"Well, somebody's got to keep an eye on you. How are you feeling?"

He shrugged.

"The climate, you know —"

"Yes, I understand. It must be difficult."

He noticed drops of rain upon her long eyelashes — they made her eyes seem brighter than before. She really was a very beautiful woman — and one day that beauty would fade, would decay and all because the miraculous rejuvenants were beyond these people's grasp. Such neglect seemed criminal. Back home her beauty would last for a century or more. Here, on this worthless world, it would be doomed in a few short years.

"Try one of these, Damian."

He roused out of the creeping mental fog that was threatening to betray him and looked down at the bundle of dark red grapes in her hand.

"They're delicious," she said.

She had called him by his first name and for some reason that helped him to feel better. But his stomach protested the prospective invasion of the small fruits.

"No — thank you. Really, I couldn't eat another thing."

"Not even one — just to try? They really are tasty."

Reflections of coloured, flashing lights danced in her dark eyes.

"All right," he groaned. "But just one."

He picked one of the grapes awkwardly — his limbs were becoming unresponsive; he really should have brought some anti-intoxicants with him — and placed it into his mouth. He closed his teeth around it cautiously and felt the juice spurt out and bite his tongue, the pulpy flesh collapse. Whatever flavour it possessed was pleasant enough but dulled by the amount of rich food and wine he had previously consumed.

67

"I think," he began and swallowed, "I've had a little too much of — everything."

"No more wine?"

"No. Too much of that, too."

But it was more than that — it was the warmth of all these happy bodies around him, the rising humidity and the weakening euphoria — he felt drowsy. He wanted to sleep and in fact he must have slipped off then into a quiet, unfussed doze without really noticing how tired he was. He awoke later with a start and found himself alone.

Rachel had disappeared and he was in darkness. Somebody had extinguished all but a few of the festive lights and the remaining ones were so distant that they shed no light upon him.

He sat up at once, confused. His head gave a lurch that matched a similar movement in his stomach, and he dared not get up for fear of shaming himself.

He looked closely around him. The guests had moved back from the patio and congregated in a semicircle between him and the house. The patio blazed suddenly with light and he realized that their attention was directed that way and not toward him. He relaxed.

He heard a far-off roll of drums or some such percussive instrument. His ears pricked up. A number of people had moved out onto the black and white tiled mosaic of the patio. They were dressed differently from the others. The women wore long flowing white gowns and the men white pants suits, intricately embroidered. Their faces were hidden by what he considered to be some sort of ceremonial masks, and there was no sound now other than the swish-swish of the women's skirts on the tiles.

The drums had ceased.

The people moved to what appeared to be predetermined positions on the patio. Others, clad more discreetly in sombre capes and cowls, assumed their places in the background. Marnsworth saw that they carried with them a variety of instruments, although he could not recognize any of them from memory.

The patio light dimmed and the masked figures in the foreground were picked out one at a time by individual spotlights. The guests crowded surreptitiously closer. A sudden hush descended upon the clearing. The dance, play or whatever it was, was about to begin.

IV

Marnsworth could not move — his curiosity had transfixed him. He could not understand what was happening. But if his mind could make no sense out of what was going on he found his body reacting to a stimulus he could not identify.

The performance seemed to be a subtle blend of mime and dance and drama juxtaposed, moving smoothly and intricately from one form to the other as the needs of the composer were answered. The music was predominantly percussive — the delicate tremor of something like castanets, muted gongs, tabors and other instruments were quite alien to Marnsworth's ears but not to his body — his cells remembered when his conscious mind did not. The general effect was hypnotic, not upon his mind so much as on his body. Although he recognized only a word here and there — or a gesture or two — he became alarmed at the way his pulse throbbed and his forehead ached. The moving figures on the mosaic dazzled and blinded him and yet he could not turn away for fear of missing something profound.

He had no idea of how long the performance lasted — time ceased to have any dominion for the duration of the play. But inevitably the dancers/actors brought the drama/dance to a close. They performed a rich and intricate coda and then moved quietly back to their original positions. A final murmur came from the hidden drums, muted and in rapport with the night, and then the spotlights dimmed. Silence and darkness rushed down upon the clearing. For perhaps a full minute nobody seemed to breathe. Then the players shed their masks and robes and moved back among the guests.

The lights returned gradually and, even when they were fully on, were somewhat duller than before. Marnsworth found that he could not easily dispel the feelings that the play had conjured up within his unsuspecting body. His eyes searched for Rachel and found her the centre of an admiring number of guests. Her eyes flashed triumphantly as they met his. She smiled and waved, turned to say something to her husband.

Childers stepped toward him. His eyes were bright with happiness.

"Well, did you like it? Rachel excelled herself tonight."

And he knew then why he had followed the movements of one of the dancers with such intensity.

"She's been working on that performance for months. Ages of rehearsals and tonight — a triumph."

"But I didn't understand a word of it," the spaceman protested.

Childers smiled graciously.

"You weren't supposed to. Latin is a rather dead language even at home — but it has a certain beauty of its own, don't you agree? Of course the Service finds little enough use for it."

He had not meant the words to cut so deep, but Marnsworth bled.

"Do you delight in your obscurity?"

"No. We try to be simple, to be close to life, to what is real. Why must the simple always seem complex to an outsider?"

Later there was a ceremony. The guests collected in the main room of Murray's house at a great wooden table. When they had arranged themselves in a reverent group around this symbol — with Marnsworth well to the rear the better to watch the ritual — Murray Wiseman came in. In his arms were several dozen books, odd little printed volumes such as the spaceman had only seen previously in out-of-the-way museums. Murray deposited the books carefully on the table and stepped back.

"Well, there's the latest batch," he announced. "Hot off the little old press. Now don't stand there all night — step forward."

And they did. Each in turn went forward and accepted, with thanks, one of the slim volumes. Childers' turn came around. He brought back a book and handled it with delight.

"Some poems of Robert Graves'," he explained.

Marnsworth said nothing.

Presently he made himself ask, "Does this little ritual round out every party?"

He was unable to conceal his contempt for useless labour.

"Whenever he's launching a new publication — yes. It takes him about three months for him to research and transcribe a new tape, then set up the type and run off each page."

"You mean he prints everything by hand?"

"Of course."

"The man's a fool."

Childers said nothing, only smiled his enigmatic smile and fondled the small book in his hands.

A solitary volume was left on the great wooden table. Murray leaned over, picked it up with a flourish. He held it briefly aloft.

"And this one's mine."

An undercurrent of laughter moved through the room and the guests began to disband. The major business of the evening was over and Marnsworth could detect the movements of people wondering whether or not it was late enough to go home — or if there might be time for one more drink.

He was intolerably weary on the way back to Childers' house. The thirty-two-hour Hydrian day, coupled with overindulgence in native food and wine, had combined to intensify his exhaustion. But once they were home Rachel brewed some of the rich dark coffee he had come to associate with the island — strange, but he could no longer think that it belonged to the Service — and this helped to revive his sagging spirits.

The two men sat apart in the main living room, sipping their warm drinks while Rachel plucked out haunting, timeless melodies on a strange stringed instrument in her lap. The instrument was broad and long and she had to sit crosslegged on the floor to play it. The fragmented music that leapt from her fingertips was unbearably ancient. The unfamiliar tonal idiom — could it have been Asian? — moved restlessly through Marnsworth's cluttered mind.

They sat thus for some time, until the stark, uncompromising music stopped and Marnsworth saw that Childers' wife had fallen asleep over her instrument. Her head was resting against the side of the divan and her dark hair was undone and pooling around her shoulders.

Childers apologized for the lateness of the affair and, with a gentleness Marnsworth envied, picked up his wife and cradled her in his arms. She did not stir.

"I guess it's time we were all asleep," Childers said. He brushed his bushy cheek against Rachel's jet-black hair. "Take any room you like."

He watched them move out through one of the doorless exits and when he walked through the house to find a place to sleep he found that a heavy weight had attached itself to his already overburdened heart.

He discovered a small, sparsely furnished room with a bed in one corner. He sank down gratefully, conscious of the spartan nature of the upholstery, but too tired to care. He felt warm; he had no need for blankets. He waved his hands across the nearby wall until it passed over the eye that controlled the light; the room dimmed down to an agreeable twilight, and finally, over a period of perhaps several minutes, into darkness.

His thoughts tumbled over and over in his muddled head, like playful kittens with sharp claws and strange music echoed around the ghostly caverns of his soul.

He thought of Rachel, and all the other women he had known, and found that sleep was elusive for a time; and when he did stumble eventually into that realm, he dreamed a nightmare . . .

Under him the world turned, breathed and pulsed with life. He lay spreadeagled and naked across it, held there by some powerful and unseen force — it was like being fastened to a medieval rack and being unable to see his tormenters. Overhead the stars wheeled crazily, burning whorls of light knitted together by shuttling steel shapes.

He felt a little like Gulliver on the island of Lilliput, bound by invisible threads to the soil beneath him.

And he was afraid. His body ached. The ache corkscrewed into agony. The force that held him inert seemed also to be pulling him down, a little at a time — down into the moist and suffocating surface of the world. He couldn't move and faces danced before him, vague and unsmiling and riddled with age. The world turned again and again and again and the rack tightened until it seemed that his body would fly apart. The angry soil rose up all around him and crept over his limbs — it wanted to bury him. His skin began to slough away from his features and he knew that a ragged, ancient face stared up at the whirling universe, where fireflies of starlight buzzed and the little steel shapes knitted busily.

He opened his mouth to cry out.

And awoke.

And found that he could not move.

The lost echo of a scream reverberated around the narrow room.

His breathing was coarse and irregular. His body weighed a ton or more. The residue of a nightmare was reluctant to let go of him. For a moment he wondered if he were really awake.

Why couldn't he move?

There was a terrible ache in his head. His face seemed to be on fire. A hundred tiny needles were burrowing through his sinus cavities. He could hardly breathe, let alone cry out, and the terrifying stigmata of his dream still glared at him out of the darkness.

His body felt dirty and uncomfortable from the burden of his sweat.

Gradually his fear subsided. He managed to roll over onto his side down to the hard wooden floor. He felt drugged — probably from too much native wine — and his movements were sluggish. But somehow he groped his way awkwardly through the dark and back into the main room, where a soft night light still glowed.

He found his suit and managed to crawl back into it. The effort seemed to take hours. His fingers scrabbled anxiously at his belt controls. Once they were functioning he leaned back against a chair and waited for some comfort to return.

The tiny mechanisms whirred audibly in the unnatural silence, busily whisking impurities out of his air. He sat still for some time — until he could breathe with some freedom — and then made his way back to his room. He sank back onto the bed exhausted.

His suit soothed and protected him and made him comfortable and he was soon fast asleep. His head stopped throbbing and the ache in his sinuses eased a little. But his dreams were vague and uncertain, although they lacked the virulence of the earlier nightmare.

He awoke with a hangover. His body was cool and comfortable but inside he felt foul. Too much incautious wining and dining had had their way — he really should have been more careful. His mouth was dry and felt like the bottom of a bird cage. He had to get a drink somewhere and something to get rid of the hangover.

There was nobody about when he walked into the main room. He opened the front door and strode to where his skiff was parked. He opened the locker and fumbled for some tablets that would alleviate the worst effects of the wine. He could not swallow them dry, so he wandered around the grounds until he found a small natural fountain around one side of the house. He cupped one hand under a faucet and washed down the pills with several ounces of fresh water.

The liquid stung his throat, it was so cold. But the flavour was not unpleasant and in a few moments he felt the veil of fog begin to lift from his mind. Yet there was a stain that refused to shift and made him feel a stranger to himself.

Too much wine, far too much. I must be more careful. That was a damned foolish thing to do . . .

He switched on his sensors and listened to the quiet. The morning was calm. Only the distant patient passage of the river moving over some rocks was audible. He extended a hand and saw a drifting film of fine rain collect upon it. Strange, he had not noticed it was raining until now. How had he come to accept something so unfamiliar?

Behind some nearby trees he spied a small stream running down towards the river. Farther on he could see where it formed a wide, shaded pool before going again about its business. Some fresh sounds came from this direction. They could have been human voices. Marnsworth ambled over in that direction to see who it was.

The pool was wide, deep and dark where the wan sunlight had not yet penetrated. Somebody was splashing happily in the chill waters. He saw an upraised arm settle back into the pool and draw the swimmer towards him.

Childers' wife — enjoying her own remedy for hangovers, he surmised. But the spaceman shivered at the thought of that icy pool and was not tempted.

He took a step forward to call out and then froze, his hands stiff at his sides. A sudden enchantment had settled over the pool. It seemed to sweep up from the past — from his past — from the unquarried limbo of his youth to a time when he, too, had swum without questions in waters no different from these. Long ago — on a world called Earth, when there had been time for such pleasures and space to accommodate them. His ears filled with the tingle of forgotten sounds and sights.

Rachel stood up and waded ashore. She stood with her feet braced wide apart and raised both her hands to her neck and crushed the cold pool from out of her long dark hair. It raced down the arch of her spine and splashed around her ankles. Her brown body was beautiful in the soft morning sunlight and Marnsworth felt a sudden and intense surge of sexual desire — so powerful that it caught him unprepared and made him shake so much that he had to lean against a nearby tree for support.

She had closed her eyes while she swept the water from her hair. Now she opened them and looked across at him, as though seeing him for the first time. And for the space of that drawn-out moment Marnsworth felt that all his life, all of his living, all that he had ever been and ever hoped to be, was stretched out between them like a finely strung wire. The silence was tangible.

And then she smiled, and flicked her hair with her hands, and stepped forward to pick up a towel. The violent need that had momentarily gripped Marnsworth quivered and then dissipated itself throughout his body. He opened his mouth but found that he could not speak. His heart hammered and pushed his blood at such a pace that it seemed to scour his lungs. He could not move or speak, for her smile had transfixed him. It had been an expression so complete in its friendship that he wondered how he could ever speak to her again. In a moment she had seen the clumsy betrayal of his face, had divined in that small space of time the nature of his desire and, with her smile, seemed to have suggested that, had the moment been otherwise, they might have lain together and she would have taken from him that terrible surge of passion. She had understood.

She moved about, drying herself, the swing of her broad hips casual and unselfconscious.

"Good morning, Damian," she said, brightly. "Sleep well?"

He could not answer. Instead he looked away and stared into the deepest part of the pool, as if the shadows of the overhanging trees could hide his shame.

A sudden splash came from the other side of the pool.

Childers' body broke the water. He swam across with slow, powerful strokes and jumped lightly ashore. He grabbed for his own towel and attacked his streaming wet body vigorously.

"Hope you slept well, Damian."

"After — a fashion," the spaceman managed. He gestured awkwardly at his survival suit. "I had to — you see."

They understood.

Rachel brushed idly at her wet hair with her towel. It was suddenly a vivid blaze of orange, the colour of the shift he had first seen her in.

Childers gave her a playful pat on the belly. "How is he this morning?"

She smiled mysteriously.

"Rachel's having a child, you know," Childers explained. "Another five months and —"

But Marnsworth wasn't listening — he had recoiled in horror, his eyes fastened on the woman's abdomen. Of course she was statuesque but he could see right away that the slight bulge at her waist was not right.

He looked like a man who had been physically struck. He stumbled a few steps backward.

"You mean — you mean she's going to have it herself?"

A cloud passed over his friend's face. Childers put his arm around his wife.

"Does that sound so strange? That my wife will have a child, from her own womb, and in her own time? That's the way she wants it, Damian — and that is the way I will be proud to accept my son — or daughter, as the case may be. You see, we won't really know until the child is born. Isn't that marvellous? For us there can't be any other way."

Marnsworth stared at them. Except for the profound and confident glow of intelligence in their eyes they looked like two naked savages. There was no longer any point in maintaining a facade of communication. Last night should have been a warning. This whole trip had been a mistake.

Without another word he spun around and marched blindly back toward his skiff. He did not know that his eyes were filled with tears — for him tears were an unaccustomed occurrence. He no longer noticed the rain and he did not hear Childers' wife calling out to him. He moved in the grip of a mindless fury. There could be nothing beyond the final proof of this insanity — it was monstrous that Childers should allow his wife to risk her life giving birth to a child in such an un-Controlled and dangerous manner.

He climbed clumsily into the skiff and swung shut the canopy. But he hesitated before the controls — they had become a hazy blur to him — and that was time enough for Childers to catch up with him. Rachel ran behind her husband, the orange towel trailing like a forlorn sail.

Marnsworth shook his head but the haze would not clear. Angrily he flicked a toggle. The motor hummed into life.

Beyond the canopy he could see Childers' face upturned and could read the despair that was etched there.

"Damian," he called out. "Damian — think of us. Think of why you came here if you never have before. We need somebody to understand — somebody to bridge the gap —"

And then they were gone. The skiff accelerated sharply skyward. It hovered for a moment, rechecking co-ordinates, and then shot away at a steep angle, allowing Marnsworth a last glimpse of the people below.

They both seemed so small, locked together in their madness. Rachel's towel made a dark orange stain on the grass. The image burned itself deep into his memory and he knew that he would never be able to erase it from his mind.

Damn you! *Damn you . . .*

The skiff moved rapidly away from the estate, burrowing anxiously through the dense rain clouds at maximum acceleration. But as fast as it moved it was pursued by something faster — a nameless invisible terror that seemed to possess the shape of a great bird of prey, vengeful and demented. It spread wide its dreadful claws and fastened them into his skull and began to tear away at his gibbering mind. Darkness engulfed him, a darkness where his voice became a whimpering pale thing that could not be heard.

The auto-pilot carried him safely back to the *Barain*, where kind hands lifted his weeping, twitching body from the small craft and carried him to a private room on board the massive starship. And there he was confined with his sickness while they fired the engines for the short passage home.

And still his terror possessed him. A stranger walked the wailing corridors of his mind — someone alien and yet himself, struggling to break free. Sometimes he awoke from his tormented dreams and struck his fists against the bulkhead until they bled, or until others arrived and strapped him back into his bed. They could not understand that he had only screamed defiance at the hostile universe outside that was crowding to get in. And he dreamed of rivers and trees and sunlight and the pallid women of Earth with their mouth agape for orgasm — but their minds were divorced in time from the simple pleasure of their bodies. They were old and yet they were young and he hated them for it and the angry beast inside him struggled to get out and smash their smiling faces. He dreamed of flesh and steel, darkness and light and his small room fogged up like the world he remembered as Island One. The same moist air draped itself around him. It was like living again in the warm wet womb he had never known. He was a child of a silver cylinder — but his cells remembered.

And Rachel's face would sometimes come smiling through the corruption and the terror and he would recall her nature and all the other things about the island and the memory would often make him smile in his sleep. Almost he began to understand. But it was only when his body took over the unequal task and remembered what it was that he had to remember, to survive, that he began to hope. But that came later.

When the physicians on Earth had finished with him. After they had nursed him and nurtured him and purged the poisons from his system. After they had slain the great ugly bird and removed its talons from his soul and then, convinced that they had done all that they could to help him, released him.

To wander lonely and afraid through the crowded streets, pushing his way through the bland unsmiling multitudes of the forever young, looking for the miracle of an old and tired face.

And for himself.

THE KITTEN

Stephen Cook

The cat belonged to Mr. and Mrs. Gordon Horner, childless. Its kittens, therefore, also belonged to Mr. and Mrs. Gordon Horner, especially since it had produced them under false pretences.

"I'm damned if I would have fed it," said Mr. Horner, "if I'd known it was a female."

He took the kittens out to the shrubbery at the bottom of the garden, where they would not disturb his wife, and dropped them into a bucket of water. They swam strongly. He left them there.

Just before dark, Mrs. Horner said, "Will you feed the cat, dear, or shall I?"

"Neither of us will feed the cat," replied Mr. Horner. "The cat has deceived us, Emily. It must find new benefactors."

"And the kittens?"

"I'll bury them now. The roses stand to benefit most from them, don't you think?"

"Gordon, you didn't!"

When he arrived again at the bucket, he found that one of the kittens had not yet given up the struggle. In fact, it hardly seemed to have tired at all. It circled the bucket steadily. The ripples thrown out by its tiny paddling paws and its probing nose lapped gently over the bodies of its brothers and sisters.

He fished out the dead ones and dropped them into a hole beside the roses.

Two days later, he remembered to look in the bucket again. There the kitten was, still swimming strongly. Its baby eyes turned up to him. Plucky little bastard, he thought; it probably can't even see yet. He left it there.

"The cat still comes to the back door for its dinner," said Mrs. Horner, several days later.

"Then why do you feed it?"

"I don't. I think it must have found somewhere else to eat, but it keeps coming back for more."

"I'll give it two more days," said Mr. Horner.

He gave it two more days, then carried it down the garden by the scruff of the neck and dropped it in the bucket. It was a bucket big enough to hold a cat, as well as kittens. Any bucket will do for kittens, but a bucket that will keep an agile, full-grown cat out of its depth is something to be really proud of. The kitten was still circling steadily.

The next day, Mr. Horner went to bury the corpse. Somehow he knew that the kitten would still be alive, yet he could not suppress a slight feeling of shock when he actually saw it. After burying the cat, he took the kitten in the bucket up to the house. Set in the side wall was a trapdoor that opened into a space under the floor. He used it for storing old pieces of timber and galvanized iron that might come in handy someday. It would be ideal for keeping the kitten out of harm's way until it decided to let itself drown. Brushing aside some of the dusty cobwebs, he set the bucket on the mouldy earth and shut the door.

A fortnight later, his curiosity got the better of him. He looked once more into the bucket. The kitten peered up at him and mewed feebly. It had grown no bigger, but, on the other hand, neither had it slowed down.

At dinner that evening, he mentioned the subject to his wife. "Darling," he began, "do you remember those kittens I drowned a month ago?"

"Of course, dearest."

"Well, one of them is still swimming."

"In the bucket?"

"I've kept it there for nearly a month. It simply will not drown."

"Give it time dear, give it time. Patience is a virtue."

He waited for another month before he succumbed to the desire to look again. He strolled casually to the trapdoor; now that he was ready to see the kitten again, he felt no need to hurry. Just as he began to fiddle with the padlock that held the bolt, he heard a faint miaow from the other side. Sighing deeply, he went to tell his wife.

"Use the axe," she suggested.

"I wouldn't have the heart."

"Then there's nothing to do but be patient for a while longer."

He decided to wait for at least six months. No kitten could swim without food or rest for six months. He placed a careful red cross on the calendar in the kitchen to mark the final day, and then, very gradually, forgot the whole thing. Six months passed, but he had forgotten what was meant by the cross. Soon it was winter, and there were three successive mornings when it was so cold that water froze in the pipes. That was most unusual, and the newspapers reported that the temperature was almost at a record low. In spring, the roses grew rapidly. Mrs. Horner entered them in a local rose show, but they did not win a prize.

"Better luck next time, dear," he consoled her. "I'll take you out to dinner tonight, instead."

They went out to dinner. It was a very nice dinner, and on the way home in the car Mrs. Horner literally purred with satisfaction.

"Good heavens," exlaimed Mr. Horner, "that reminds me."

But Mrs. Horner chose this moment to suggest that he help her win next year's rose show, by buying her a particular new variety that was very rare, very beautiful and very expensive. In bed that night, he remembered that he had remembered something, but could not remember what it was.

He bought the new rose, but not until after another year

had brought yet another failure in the show. Mrs. Horner accepted it graciously and asked for his assistance in planting it.

"We'll need a stake to tie it to," she said.

"I'll get one from under the house."

"Oh, there's no need — I think I left one behind the shrubbery some time ago."

Mr. Horner went down to the shrubbery to find the stake. While he was there, he remembered that he had once drowned some kittens and a cat. There was something more, but he could not quite place it. He carried the stake back up through the garden.

"There's no need for you to stay out here," said Mrs. Horner. "I'll put the stake in myself."

He thanked her and went inside, to her secret chagrin and his own secret pleasure, since they both knew that she had not expected to be taken at her word. Some time later, she asked him for the key to the trapdoor under the house. The stake had broken, and she had to find another. He gave it to her with cheerfulness and a thick skin, but something began nagging at his memory. It bothered him so much that he had to lay down his newspaper and think about it.

Of course! The kitten! He sprang from his comfortable chair and hurried outside, in time to see his wife emptying the bucket. The kitten lay beside her on the grass, panting rapidly, its legs twitching in an automatic parody of the motions of swimming. It had not grown a millimetre.

"Gordon!" she exclaimed. "Something incredible has happened."

"I know, dear," he said nervously. "The kitten."

"I'd forgotten all about it."

"So had I. Was it still swimming?"

"It had almost stopped, but most of the water had evaporated, and I think it might have been able to last until the bucket was dry." She had begun to scrape out the sides of the bucket with soil. "You really should have looked at it long ago. The water was filthy, absolutely filthy. I don't know how the poor thing could stand it."

"I'm sorry, I forgot all about it. The muck seems to come off fairly easily. Here, let me give you a hand."

"No, don't bother. I'm almost through." She carried the bucket to a tap among the flowers and filled it again.

"What are you doing now?" he asked.

"Putting it back under the house, of course. What's the alternative?"

"Well . . . I thought, you know . . ."

"Have you changed your mind about keeping it?"

"No, of course not," he replied quickly.

"Then you've either got to drown it, or put the axe to it."

"I'm damned if I'll use the axe on any animal!"

"And neither will I. It isn't a woman's job at all. Don't worry — Puss won't be able to outlast this bucketful. Surely not!"

"Do you think we might be able to give it away?"

Mrs. Horner looked down her nose at the tiny animal. She sniffed. "It doesn't exactly look handsome, you know."

"We can clean it up — give it a bath, or . . ."

"Drying it out would be more to the point, Gordon, or was that your idea of a joke?"

"Heavens, no! How could I laugh at such a poor creature?"

They gave the kitten time to dry itself in the sun. Soon it came looking for food. They gave it two saucers of warm, sugared milk before it was satisfied. Mr. Horner, mentally calculating its diet on a weight-for-age basis, foresaw it eating them out of house and home. He hoped they would not have to keep it for long.

"The biggest danger of all," he confided to his wife, "is that it will come to think of this place as its home — like its mother."

"It's too young for that," she replied.

On the next afternoon, Mrs. Anthony Hines paid a visit. Mrs. Horner, her husband being at the office, took it upon herself to present the cat.

"Oh, no, my goodness gracious me, no!" said Mrs

Hines. "I'm allergic to cats!"

"Such smooth, slinky animals, don't you think?" said Mrs. Horner.

"The word isn't slinky, Emily, it's sneaky. I don't mind dogs, but I would never, Emily, never trust my life to a cat."

"But does one ever find it necessary to do such a thing?" asked Mrs. Horner.

"Don't *ask* such things. The very look of the animal is enough to tell you. There's only one thing a cat asks from you. Comfort. Food and warmth, Emily, that's the only part of you and your home that it cares for. I don't care what they say in the biology books, dear, I know that cats are completely cold-blooded. Like fish."

"How odd you should say that," said Mrs. Horner, and told her something of the kitten's history. Mrs. Hines showed a quickened interest. Encouraged by this unaccustomed attention, Mrs. Horner went on in more detail.

"You don't say," breathed Mrs. Hines. "How very curious. It's really too absurd. And you really want me to take it, for nothing, right now? Why, I couldn't look myself in the eye ever again if I refused. Of course I'll take it off your hands, Emily dear. I'd do anything for you — you know that."

And Mrs. Horner, who was just beginning to wonder if she ought to keep the kitten after all, found that she had it no longer.

When Mrs. Hines left, she invited the Horners to a dinner party which she planned to give in a fortnight's time. Mrs. Horner told her husband in the evening, and they both looked forward to the occasion. Mrs. Hines threw magnificent dinner parties.

The arrangements were as splendid as the Horners had expected. Mrs. Hines led them to a small group of strangers who proved most congenial, then made certain that they did not stagnate there all night. One of the secrets of her success was that she did not allow time for messy "deep" conversations to develop. At the proper moment, she led her guests into the dining room. The Horners' pleasure was only slightly diminished by the discovery that the centrepiece of the table was an enormous fishbowl. Swimming smoothly around inside the bowl was the kitten.

"Naughty, naughty," cried Mrs. Hines, patting a tipsy guest on the hand as he reached for the bowl. "I'm sorry, but you mustn't take her out. I've got to insist upon that, you do understand? As soon as you take her out, she starts to grow."

INCUBATION

John Romeril
& Damien Broderick

He strode like some Cinerama hero in the teeth of a gale, big, relaxed, his grin wide and brilliant. He walked as though the street were there for him, and him alone. At a corner news-stand he bought a morning paper.

He wended his way to the park, relaxed on a favourite wrought-iron bench under the serrated shade of an elm, flicked through the paper. The glaring headline was barely worth a glance: GIANT CHINESE TEST TIPPED. Christ, he thought, the money they squander on ways to kill themselves. He growled in uninterested disgust, turned to the Personal Columns and the business of living.

Four lines leapt up for attention. *Rogel*, he read, *everything different now. Situation finally under control, but we must go. Meet midday, Kings X library. Silver.*

Soame passed his tongue over dry lips, felt the old excitement flutter through his body. This one was perfect. He knew it was perfect, without knowing why it was, or how he knew it.

He reached the library with thirty minutes to spare.

Practically deserted as the place was, he knew already that their eyes were caressing him. A plump spinster peered from her pimpled face between the catalogues. And — ah! the youngest of them stared from the desk with an unashamed innocence that fluted in his blood. She was no more than seventeen. As one would approach a doe, gently, he crossed to her. There was plenty of time to indulge his taste, in part at least, before the fated Silver arrived.

You lucky girl, thought Clive Hymes Soame, holding her eyes as he approached, *you beautiful young thing.*

He touched the desk, bent slightly to her. A fine veined throat, delicate copper, inspired the connoisseur in him. She swallowed prettily.

'Yes, sir?' — her soft startled voice. 'Can I help you?'

'I hope so,' and the growl was deep from use, a warmth that enfolded her. 'I'm anxious to see some of Patrick White's novels. You see, I've not been here long, yesterday in fact, from Paris.' He let his voice stroke the city's name, evoke the voluptuous mad-wild Paris that hardly exists in reality. And a wisp of illusion caught in her sigh.

Soame smiled engagingly. 'I heard nothing but praise for his work in New York. It seems a nice way to fill out my new experience of Australia, by looking at some of your best literature.'

'Of course,' she managed, still trapped in the net of his brilliant smile. She glanced nervously behind her; the old spinster was not watching them. 'Well,' she said, slipping out from behind the desk, 'I think I can offer you a special surprise.' A door marked *Private* opened for her and he followed, aglow with the old satisfaction.

They came into a dim inlet bay of books, a small hidden atoll of jutting shelves and covered tables.

'The library is preparing a public exhibition of Mr. White's work,' she whispered. 'Here, in fact, we have all his original manuscripts . . . ' Her voice trailed away.

With the air of a world-weary expert, Soame let his eyes drift from books to manuscripts to holograms and tapes. The girl's fresh, animal body pervaded his nostrils with the scent of lust. Vulnerable as a puppet, she waited for firm direction from the strings.

'Fascinating,' he husked, casually replacing a first-edition of *The Aunt's Story.* 'Of course, the insight which literature can offer is ultimately less significant than that which one gains through *people*, the immediate relationships, the role of chance . . . ' He trailed off, as if reflecting on the thread woven by fate through jetsetting travels. And, after all, there was a thread. With him, crowding his mind, were all the women of his past, the Silver of his future, and this delightful creature of the moment. It was that blend called experience.

'Yes,' she breathed. 'Ah, um, here's an unbound copy of Mr. White's new novel . . . ' She reached up towards the volume, slender arm shaping the light fawn of her sweater. Soame watched her breasts shift and hungered for them. With a trembling hand she offered him the book. He took it, brushing her hand.

'Can I, uh, anything else?' Her breath came in short stabs.

'Thank you, dear,' he murmured, 'no, this has been excellent.'

But he did not move. Close to her face, he held strings of suspense. And he slipped down to her alluring mouth, lifting her face. Full, warm, fired, he structured their lips in a damp unison, an erotic geometry. Angles, tensions tugged her into the whirlpool. His hand lured her arm, smothered her young breast. A shiver rippled her dress.

It pleased him. He had made her alive, everywhere alive, everywhere his. Through her scent, a dewy freshness shook him into an echo of memories.

'My dear,' he said, bending to her face, 'you must have dinner with me some —' But her eyes had skittered away from him, stared in near-terror into the cool reprimand of the plump spinster who stood at the opened door.

'I — I hope this has helped you,' the girl stammered, not daring to meet his gaze. 'I'd best, better go.' And she scurried off with burning cheeks.

It did not really upset Soame. He glanced at his watch, moved smoothly back into the body of the library. Still, he would have enjoyed playing the little drama out. The old prude waddled past, and Soame regarded her with cold contempt. She dropped her wrinkled eyes to her wrinkled breast, and he laughed silently, cruelly. She winced, hating his beautiful body, and fled behind the catalogues.

Lunch-hour borrowers had begun to file into the library. Casually, he made his way among them, searching the faces. The woman, his instinct told him, had not yet arrived. His was a precarious game, he thought idly; against time rather than the two other abstract personalities involved. If Silver were late his scheme was lost, blown, just as it would be if the oddly-named Rogel were to come early.

As the clock sliced seconds from the hour, tension paced like a beast he knew and respected. He savoured his controlled fear, tasted it, let the honed edge of habit cut away all superfluous thought.

And she was there.

From the corner of his eye, he saw the woman enter, captured and analysed without conscious effort the minute keys of stance and attitude which identified her. He breathed evenly, coiled the tension back on itself and closed it away. A clear flexible mind was the prime necessity of this moment; he needed to sum up her character, attune himself to her. He slid unobtrusively forward. Before anything else, he had to gauge her financial status.

Yet even his experienced clarity had not been prepared for her. The stunning fabulous beauty of the woman brought him up short. Stupid fumbling fingers reached for a cigarette. *A library, fool*, he snarled at himself, dismayed at the near-blunder. Gingerly, struggling for lost composure, he approached her.

'Silver?' he murmured softly. *Rogel's emissary*, urged the posture of his body, the angle of his arm, the carefully-weighed values of his tone. The role was merging with his own instincts and memories, a sense of conviction which came straight from sinew and bone.

"Yes?" she said, voice hushed, puzzled. Somewhere in her tone, anxiety raced. But in the half-gloom a radiance remained in her pale features, an ultimate firm confidence. 'Where is Rogel? There is not time to alter the arrangements.'

Arrangements. Was this an assignation? A return to a husband? A business matter? The possibilities gridded themselves like a chessboard. Somehow he would have to get the details, or he was lost.

'Regrettably,' Soame said, projecting calm capability, 'there has arisen the need for a small change of plan. I'm here to —' He swept his eyes around the library, lowered his voice still more. 'Look, we can't really talk here. Best we go and talk over coffee. I'll give you a full account then.'

She nodded reluctantly. 'We'll go,' she said, 'to my apartment.' An odd smile touched her lips as she glanced about her. At what? The people, the books? Her English had been too perfect. Her face, too, was perfect, a faultless masterpiece of femininity which defied classification. *Where is she from?* demanded his disciplined mind. There was so much he needed to know.

Gently, he took her arm and guided her to the door. They stepped outside into a cool wind, and drifting leaves lapped their feet. Amost sluggishly, his stunned mind tried to reckon her wealth. Never had there been less cause for worry on that count. Silver passed his test of affluence easily. Better still, in the lack of ostentation about her deep topaz brooch, couched in simple exquisite silver work, there was nothing of the suspicious, flashy *nouveau riche.* Her plain tweed jacket impressed Soame — not the material, nor the way it tastefully pronounced firm breasts; the cut spoke eloquently of high-priced fashion. There was the same classic purity in the woollen dress which fell, in the current mode, just above her knees.

Playful wind tossed at her hair, and she lifted sensitive fingers to push back an errant lock. Her hand — jewelled with a single sparkling diamond — her arm, in its wide half-length sleeve, her graceful body inflamed his imagination. Here was the opportunity of a lifetime: money, beauty, grace. Quickly, hand barely at her elbow, Soame guided her to a taxi. Determinedly, he slammed the cab door, settled into the upholstery.

They sat for five minutes in silence while the cab

threaded through snarling traffic. A rustle of nyloned knee, a twist of tweed, brought her around to face him. Aesthetic appraisal, appreciation moved her face. With a touch of real pleasure, Soame watched the slight smile which curved her lips. *We're two of the same breed,* he thought: *the beautiful people.*

'What are you calling yourself?' she asked, her voice a song. And it was there again, Soame noted. He could not place the foreign quality.

'I'm Clive,' he said. 'Clive Hymes Soame, from the old world, newly of Australia.' Always, even with a woman seemingly as beyond pretension as this lovely Silver, it paid to get Europe into the picture.

She laughed, a tinkle of joyful melody. 'Such a complicated name.' Then, soberly: 'What of the others? Are they safely under field?'

Soame was lost and sinking. He had not the slightest idea what she was talking about.

'They are, my dear,' he said, holding her gaze, no smallest trace of hesitation in his voice. An open snare, his mind waited ready to snap down on anything which might be a key to this strange, entrancing, rich woman.

'Naturally,' she laughed, shaking her head in self-mockery. 'If they were not, we would not be here, would we?' Gravely, Soame agreed. 'And what of Rogel?' she pressed.

Abruptly, Soame knew what to say. *We must go,* her notice in the Personal Column had said, and she was obviously still anxious about something. Adding to her indefinably foreign beauty, her curiously perfect articulation, it was clear that she and Rogel and 'the others' were preparing to leave the country. *Christ, I'll have to pounce, and pounce fast.*

'As you appreciate,' he said carefully, 'the situation is precarious. Rogel felt that he ought to attend personally to final preparations.' In the pupils of her violet eyes curved the calm, urbane features Soame presented her.

'There is,' she quietly agreed, 'a great deal of urgency. Now that I've located the Egg, we must get it away before the weapon test disrupts my control.'

Ignorance sucked like a whirlpool. Soame was torn inside with terror. A single wrong word would blow the whole goddam scene. He'd waited years for such a victim. His grasping soul itched for her wealth, his jaded senses lusted for her body. And he could feel the prize slipping out of his hands . . . Sharply, he grabbed self-control.

'Let's not talk about it for the time being.' Soame indicated the cabbie, alert, efficient, listening. Again she nodded, turned away to view the passing streets. He relaxed, fought the varieties of tension in him.

Still, he couldn't resist her profile, the piquant blossoming lips which had lapsed into silence, the brow that curved uncreased into ash-white hair. The sun, cooler now in a concrete sky, burned copper into the cascade of that hair. Soame's eyes slipped back to her unblemished cheeks, smooth as satin, her fine high cheekbones that lent fragility to her spirited jaw.

A cool sweat of desire pricked out on his palms. A long life-line there, he had been told once. At this rate he would die within the hour. He forced himself back to business.

'I left Rogel at the airport making final arrangements,' That seemed safe enough. It was in all likelihood damnably close to the truth. If Silver was preparing to leave the country, hammered his mind, even the carefully prepared tale about poor Rogel's 'unfortunate accident' wouldn't hold her for long . . .

She was looking at him with incredulous amazement. He had, then, said something dreadfully wrong. His stomach butterflied, knotted.

After an intolerable silence, she laughed richly. 'Of course, dear,' she smiled, taking his hand, 'the natives. You seem to have assimilated the local humour. The quaint gigantic lying.' Her eyes shone when she laughed, bright and reassuring. Soame laughed with her, he who had laughed long and loud at the painful wit of old, horrible, redeemingly-rich widows, and he wondered what they were laughing at.

Natives. That was the key. And her foreign aura. And

the library. People do not meet in a library, even the cultivated. The answer was gnawing for attention.

Christ, yes. A scholar! No wonder he had taken so long — this beautiful, wealthy creature a scholar? *Perhaps*, Soame sketched in his mind, *she's a member of some ancient landed aristocracy, secure still in their prosperity despite the encroachments of the welfare state.* The scholar-gentry. An anthropologist, perhaps, or a sociologist.

The taxi turned against traffic, stopped before an expensive apartment block.

The apartment confirmed his evaluation of Silver, rich, rich, Silver. *Soame, you lucky devil*, he congratulated himself, *handle this right and you've got it made.* Wide latticed windows gave on to a magnificent view of Sydney Ha.'bour and the arching Bridge with its ant-like traffic. Expertly, he cased the flat: two bedrooms, kitchen, the living room where Silver busied herself at the mahogany bar. Her tweed coat was slung lazily on a low tonal purple divan. His mind kept flickering with the image she'd made against the window, slipping out of the coat as he held it: smoothing down her skirt, her head thrown back so that swirling strands had sent white fire through him. Hawk was dangerously close to becoming prey.

She turned and sang a melody of gay gibberish.

Mental snares snapped tight, held for Soame the knowledge that these were words in a language he had never heard before. In the frozen moment of panic, he raised his eyebrows in mock reproach.

'Let us use the local language,' he scolded, and the touch of whimsy in his reproof was staggeringly adroit. 'It has its own amusing charm.' *Dear God, did I really say that, without hesitation, with only my reflexes to guide me?*

Her lips quirked in acknowledgement. 'Will whiskey do?' she asked. 'For a laugh, as they say. It's growing cool.'

'Fine with me.' Soame watched her shoulders move beneath the violet blouse. 'Anything.' A brown-gold carpet

95

met deep oak walls of vertical boards to a gold and ivory wallpaper. The high ceiling was a soft, almost translucent grey. Subdued lighting touched the room with rose light that mellowed rather than dispelled the dimness. Here, he decided, under the Edwardian ceiling, amid the faded leather of old books, before the colourless seasons of Turner and Constable, he would take her.

She brought whiskey, and captivated him. Her breasts in the rose light were beautiful as she bent with glass in hand as though offering her body in some delicate exotic ritual.

'It is quaint enough, is it not?' She swirled her glass, watched red-gold fire dance.

Almost, lost in a different intoxication, he caught the incredible import of her words. *Quaint?* shrilled a distant, numbed awareness. *Scotch, quaint? Nobody can be that foreign!* But he was awash with her, and criminal artifice was lost in the darkness of his captivity . . .

'It took a little while to adapt,' she was saying. 'Still, we are an adaptable race, are we not?'

Soame nodded, clutching at the social gambit. 'Astonishing thing, the survival instinct,' he agreed. She was his gold-spoon girl of the year — of his life. If he played the right cards he could score magnificently.

The flicker of candles threw long shadows against the wall. They danced, music sweeping soft and tantalising. Soame was at ease. He had dined superbly, managed to fend off Silver's anxious questions, and now she spun before him in a chiffon twirl. It floated about her, shifting over perfect limbs. Thin wreathes of blue smoke drifted in the air from a Sobranie left burning in the ashtray. He followed the wreathes through slitted eyes: the smoke symbolised his future, the same soft lazy drift, pregnant with a poignant odour of wealth.

'Mmm,' she sighed from his chest, nuzzling his jacket. 'The sound-tape has stopped. What will we do?'

'Nothing,' growled Soame, 'nothing, my sweet, just dance.'

Long fingers unbuttoned his jacket, a slender white arm slipped along his side. He brushed with his lips the translucent glow of her arm as she traced the muscled flesh of his shoulders.

'You are lovely,' he whispered into her ash-blond hair, 'you prepare a wonderful meal, you dance like a sylph, you're more than a human being deserves to be in this vile world.'

Incredulous, she swept back her head. The pale arch of her neck ravished him even as the wonder in her gaze sent a strange fear through him. And —

'Of course!' Then: her laugh, sweet as water over pebbles. 'Ah, darling, a local saying! Your humour has bite.' Again she nestled against him, brushing his thigh.

Bewilderment misted Soame's eyes. Once more he had floundered beyond his depth. He cringed internally before the enigma she presented. What was his joke? His simple, silly words — trite banalities, utterances without significance — were suddenly yawning chasms, dangerous deeps for which he could make no preparation. Desperate, he sought the country of the mute. Her fingers were a fiery pressure, and he drew her to the divan.

Every vestige of control slipped from Soame in that moment. He was lost; for the first time in his adult life he was not the manipulator. The shock was extraordinary. He reeled toward an abyss of unknowledge, a vertigo of jumbled raw sensation. A wonderful sigh swelled in Silver's throat, flowed soundlessly through him. The pain of touch was a rainbow eruption . . .

All animation stopped. The room froze.

'No,' she cried. It was, in the terrible silence, almost a scream. It wrapped itself like concrete about his abdomen. 'What are we doing? The fields, the Egg!' Her violet eyes, as she shuddered, were filled with real terror, and she thrust Soame away from her.

Bewildered, shocked even beyond the sentimentality which had carried him near the edge of remorse, he stood gaping. Furious pressures raged inside him, as if he were a bomb held at the moment of explosion.

Her breathing slowed. 'Not yet,' she said, with surprising softness. 'Tomorrow night, when we are gone.' Her face held the sadness of happiness recalled in sorrow. 'You're too beautiful,' she moaned. 'It hurts. I'll have to turn you off.'

And her eyes seemed to glow magenta, fierce and troubled. Soame felt a new pressure, a tiny tearing agony, like some obscene torture. An icy, psychic wave grew, raced dripping wet through his blood.

Silver's cool tones, sharp and clear, echoed in the colder vault of his raped soul.

'That was dangerous, my sweet.' Smooth as marble, her beautiful features were raised to him. Somewhere, beyond the room, there was a dull ticking.

'My God,' Soame shrilled, barbs in his throat. 'Baby what happened?'

She passed a hand wearily across her brow, and her mood changed to irritation. 'You've really been an observant boy, haven't you?' she snapped, not looking at him. Her lips were pale where the muscles caught light. 'But please, I've had enough of the indigenes tonight. I'm too lonely and too vulnerable. I want home and I want you. So please —'

He didn't understand. He *could* not. What the hell was he doing standing here if she was so lonely, vulnerable? Soame eyed her with a dispassion that was incredulous, and could not deny the psychic castration she had somehow worked on him. And the anger grew, anger out of impotence and ignorance and the pain of humiliation. Blood pounded in his ears, and beyond that was the ticking, the shuddering grinding metronome which hadn't been in the room before that appalling instant.

Silver's scream, when it did come, was a terrible piercing thing of grief and the very taste of blood as it tore her throat. Her face leapt before him.

She was gone; and stood in front of him.

Blanched, she held out a black ovoid in her hands.

It riveted his eyes. It seemed to suck light from the room. It thundered in his mind with a terrible beat. He was cold and put his fingers in his mouth, and was very afraid.

She held the thing, the muscles of her arms starkly taut and they were not what held it, and the shuddering beat died away, was contained.

'What we nearly did!' Her chill voice came shaken to him. 'I ought not to have lost control, even for a moment. But I had expected to be out of this planet by now. We should already have had it in the null-field.' She turned distraught eyes on Soame. 'We *must* go to the ship now. I have lost face with the Egg; I doubt that I am capable of containing it much longer without fieldforce assistance. And we have to get it out anyway, before the megabomb finally triggers its memory.'

The words fled over Soame's mind. In terror, he pointed at the black thing she seemed to be calling the Egg. 'What is it?' he screamed. 'Christ, what *is* it?'

The woman stumbled back from him. 'No,' she howled, and he was lashed by an impact greater than the words of her mouth, 'no, you're so beautiful,' as though a rent had opened in her soul, and the furious incredulity of her very thoughts was roaring this hurricane about his mind, 'no human could be so —'

Like a badly-matched stereo, Soame saw himself against the image of Silver's face, saw, through the torrent of strangeness that poured from her opening soul into his, the transfixed stupidity in his face, his stance, caught the incomprehensible truth which smashed at her in that blurry blinding moment. 'Earthling!' she screamed. *'Worm!'*

Her hand hung before him, ripped down, furrowed, raked his flesh. He stood bleeding and dumb like a whipped mule.

'Where *is* Rogel?' she cried. It singed the edges of his consciousness, fried him until he seemed aflame in her fury. The drumming, humming beat grew again, pounded as her control slipped. 'What have you done with Rogel?'

For the eon of a minute the name clanged in his head and meant nothing, made no connection in the broken dynamo of his skull. He whimpered, and the angry beat said *Rogel Rogel Rogel* in neat bars.

'I don't know him, I never saw him, never met, never saw, never . . . ''

Silver screamed through the thunder of the Egg, an alien hysteria that brought vomit to his mouth. There was again the magenta glow in her beautiful eyes, Soames saw it despite the wild astigmatism in his clotted sight. It was more than fury, more than fear, wonderful, vast, a stature of Lear and Oedipus in those eyes, a ground-quaking, venomous, magnificent, futile torment.

'Death,' she said. She thrust the black crystalloid form at him. It hummed and glowed jet as coal. 'Death, Earthling, in cupped hands.'

The man's eyes were trapped in its blackness, his sight ruptured, for the dark thing was still and silent in her arching hand for all that it beat a crashing smashing, booming tombing convulsion that should have leapt like a heart in her naked grasp. And the edges of her soul were leaking out again, cutting through the fibres and fabric of his ravaged parts:

She looked across the street-light jewels of the city which enslaved her. Too late for Rogel to reach her. And how could he find her, now that they had missed their rendezvous? For the essence of their mission denied them the use of parasensory contact, demanded that she work alone in her cocoon of desolation until the Egg be found and restrained. And now, indeed, it was too late to bind the Egg those several days required to renew contact with Rogel and the ship, wherever in the city it was. Golden tears hung in her eyes, tears for herself and the end of immortality, tears of stupid, primitive, doomed mankind.

The flaming mosaic of her awareness fused against the fragments of Soame's shattering personality, welded them to the shape of a resonating fork to her anguish, the paradox strangeness of her reality, the sharp poignance of her resolve. He rang her dirge:

Perhaps there would be time to warn Rogel, time to have the spacecraft wrap emergency protective energies about itself. She would lay herself bare, open out her mind in one last moment of mental unity with her people. And, in the doing of it, she would perforce loosen her last tenuous psionic restraint on the Egg, permit the end of its incubation. For it would hatch at any moment. Already the megaton flare was igniting beyond the horizon, already were those barbaric scientists sending their unwitting final instruction to the Egg's pseudogenetic core, already was it beyond her endurance to contain it for any longer than mere minutes more. At least she could warn her companions.

In her hands, death hummed and glowed black as coal, and still Soame cowered in the dementia of his terror without understanding the magnitude of his final betrayal. The superhuman, poignantly-mortal creature standing above him looked down in something that was nearly pity.

'You don't realize, do you, my poor earthling slug?' Her voice was distantly calm. 'This piece of hell, this crystal Egg, this fragment of destruction from the black depths between the universes — it has lain harmless on the face of your planet for three thousand years.'

Soame whimpered, crawling in the jaws of death.

'Your bombs,' she said, 'began its incubation. We have been seeking it for twenty years on your planet, to bind it, for unconstrained it gorges on energy. It will suck your world dry, it will blacken the hot core of your green Earth. It will eat your sun,'

His voice, rough as rope: 'Who are you?'

'We are the Seekers, the Binders.' Silver's eyes filled again with remembered pain. 'Our star is far away in space and time, a twisted ember. Your world will die like ours, for I cannot hold the Egg much longer. Its nuclear enzymes have called it from sleep to a furious reawakening.'

Like a bounding, bouncing echo her voice fell into the chill eternity of frozen portraits from her soul. Soame looked as she looked at the ruined mindless animal at her feet. 'You were too perfect,' she whispered, 'too much like us to behold. And I dared not touch your mind for fear of disturbing the Egg.' The goddess made a harsh bark that was lost in the thunder of the hatching doom she held. 'I thought you were one of the young ones born on the ship while I roamed this world seeking the Egg.

'But I will warn the others.' Her eyes flared magenta flame, her lips twisted like jagged shrapnel.

Intense, shattering an instant of time, her mind speared a darkness deep as the darkness of the Egg. She found Rogel and her people (the clear tinkling minds of the new-born panged, and she knew a flooding joy in her sacrifice); they waited, puzzled and tense, in the ship.

'*Go, go,*' *Silver cried, and felt a last moment of warm, sorrowing union before crashing energies locked the starship into safety.*

There was a roaring in the room, a leaping incandescence as the Egg sucked light into itself.

And there were no human beings, there was no Earth, to see the sun give itself up.

ILLUMINATION

Michael Wilding

I

When he found himself in the valley it was already dusk; the night would descend heavily, suddenly, very soon. His glasses had broken and without them, his poor close vision combined with the dusk, he kept stumbling against things he could not see.

As soon as he saw the villagers, he stopped. He did not know who they were and was afraid of their possible hostility. In the silence, now his stumbling had ceased, he waited to hear them speak in case he knew the language. But now his stumbling had ceased, there was no sound at all. They seemed to move without sound, to perform their actions in total silence.

It was cold now and the sun was almost set. The villagers began to move back to their settlement. He strained his ears to listen, but though he saw their lips move, he could hear nothing.

II

He lay some time in the short grass at the edge of the clearing the villagers had been cultivating. He tried to estimate how much time had passed. When he thought three or so hours had elapsed, he rose and walked in the direction the villagers had taken. As he had expected, he soon came on another clearing, scattered with adobe huts — single storeyed, rough finished, but quite extensive. He looked carefully. The one nearest showed no lights; no sounds issued from it. Its doorway was open. The odds were its inhabitants were somewhere in the centre of the village; he could risk going in for food, he had to eat; and if they were inside, the hut was nearest to the edge of the clearing, and he could make his escape.

He approached it quietly, entered it carefully to brush against nothing; inside he stood stock still, straining his eyes in the dark to look round. A girl lay asleep on a mattress on the floor, covered by a blanket, except for a bare arm which she had reached from beneath it. She was beautiful but it was not the time to admire beauty. He stood still not for the beauty of her fine boned face, her rich black hair, but to make sure that he had not disturbed her. Yet her beauty entranced him all the same. And when she turned over, smiling in her sleep, at some dream, perhaps, he watched her because of her beauty.

And then she sat up. He should have left, not have stood watching her, left when he was able. She sat up, her eyes looked directly at him. He tensed himself for her scream. But she did not scream. Instead, she rose from her bed, the blanket falling away to disclose her nakedness, her full breasts, her slender waist, her slim legs. She rose and walked towards him. He had the insane fantasy that she was coming to welcome him to her bed, and he put his arm out to embrace her when she should reach him. But his arm, his hand, encountered nothing; and when she reached him, there was no contact from her rich warm nakedness, but an absurd ironic parody of love's hopeless ambition, the merging of two bodies into one. Except that this was no merging or interpenetration; merely, she occupied the same space as he did, for a brief moment, as she passed right through him, an insubstantial wraith. And it was he who screamed.

And he recoiled, backed into the wall of the hut which, instead of supporting him, offered no resistance, let him pass right through its intangible substance into the village outside. In terror he ran from the ghost village and its ghostly inhabitants, pausing occasionally to listen for them following him after his scream. But they didn't follow.

III

He woke in the morning to the sound of crickets and birds, unseen, in the bushes and trees. He had slept at last from exhaustion; but he had slept uneasily. And he was bruised and gashed from running through the dark night.

He yawned, stretched his arms out before him: and they were not there. The terror seized him again. He looked down at his feet, at his body: he was not there. Yet when he looked around, grassland was there, trees were there, a lake caught the sun's rays and glistened.

He ran, stumbling, to the lake's edge, plunged into it, felt the cool water round his invisible legs. He looked down for his reflection. But there was no reflection. Nor were there ripples when he moved.

He looked round and round: but left no shadow. Yet other objects existed; yet he existed. He could feel his hands, could clasp them; with invisible fingers he could pinch invisible flesh. He reached down to one of the round smooth stones on the lake's bed, to throw it and see if that would ripple the surface. But his hand clasped on something soft, sticky, repulsive. There were only stones to see, but his hand grasped no stones; just that stickiness from which he recoiled in horror. He looked automatically to see what he had touched, what stain it had left on his hand. But there was no hand to see.

Slowly he drew back from the lake, stood on dry land. He started to run along the stony shore. The stones gave way to huge slabs of rock, and he ran more easily than on the slipping stones that wrenched his ankles. Then suddenly he fell, plunged beneath the water, choking, struggling. He forced himself to the surface, struck out automatically with swimming motions, blinked the water from his eyes, snorted it from his nose. Yet he was not in water. He was waist deep in a slab of rock. Yet neck deep in water. His eyes saw the impalpable rock: his body felt the invisible water.

He swam an absurd breaststroke, to his eyes through air and rock, but his arms and legs carried him through the water until he grazed against some solid obstruction and, scrambling with animal terror, his eyes useless, he regained firm ground. Visual reality coincided with the tactile again: except for his body's invisibility. He lay on rock slab feeling the sun drying him. He lay there trying to understand; and afraid to move.

Somehow, from shock, from exhaustion, he lost consciousness. When he woke he froze, seeing the villagers all around him, supporting between them huge nets, standing at the lake's edge. He feared they had detected him, come to capture him. Till he realized they ignored him, seemed unaware of his presence. No doubt he was invisible to them as he was to himself.

He watched one man walk along the rock that had suddenly become water. He watched to see what would happen, like watching a man approach a banana skin. But nothing happened. The villager walked along the rock's surface, did not fall into the invisible water at all.

He was still fearful of arousing their attention, when one walked straight through him, like the girl the night before. Or not walked, but passed, glided like a wraith, a bodiless image. Walked through him not noticing him (neither of them felt anything) and joined the others by the lake with their fishing nets. When they spoke together, no sounds issued; their lips alone showed that they spoke.

V

He had never believed in ghosts, but what were they if not ghosts; but could the land be ghostly too? Was that ghost rock, those huts ghost adobe? Rocks and villagers all looked so solid, so palpable; when they touched each other, their hands did not sink through their substance, as his hands sank through.

The girl came down again: he was enthralled by her beauty, that the night before he had seen her naked. Her beauty drew his terror away again for a while. He watched her for her beauty, not for understanding: but watching her increased his understanding, watching her he became aware of something about the villagers' behaviour. They moved their hands incessantly, as if warding off objects, or guarding against collision with objects, like blind people. When he watched them closely, he saw that they never stood and looked at anything; and when two did stand still, their gaze was directly at the blazing sun. It seemed not to affect them. He saw that they were not looking, but listening to someone calling from the distance, whose hands were cupped round his mouth: the sun did not hurt their eyes, because they had no sight.

VI

He was desperately hungry. But there was no food. The villagers had brought food, fruit and fish, and a sort of bread. He crept out to steal from it, crept though he knew they could not see him. But his hands closed on emptiness. Later he watched them eat it, eat with their so solid looking bodies that so solid looking food, to him so impalpable, commenting on its qualities with lively conversation, soundless to him.

VII

He realized visual reality and tactile reality did not correspond. Or was it visual reality and tactile appearance; or visual appearance and tactile reality? How could he tell; he was loth to surrender the primacy of the visual. But his body's hunger, his bruises, pressed on him the primacy of tactile realities: the visual did not hurt him. Yet why need that make the visual only appearance? Perhaps the unhurtful was the real, the ideal; like the girl.

Occasionally, trees he saw would be there to the touch of his invisible hands. But their details would be different. It was this that brought understanding to him. He reached for the fruit of one tree. His hand clasped on soft, delicate, fragile substances that he could not see: substances that felt like flowers. He broke them away in his hand, felt them carefully. The fruit remained unplucked, impalpable. From the simple process of growth, of flowering and fruition, he realized what separated the realities, the appearances. Between the tactile and the visual was a time lag.

His sudden illumination elated him. Having reached for fruit he had found flowers: a delay of, say, six months between the tactile and the visual: light waves delayed here in their travel, no longer did they convey an immediate image. He deduced that to reach for flowers might bring him to fruit. The pattern was not so simple: for some branches he saw were not there to the touch at all; and some, invisible, bruised him when he struck against them. But he found fruit: fruit unpredictably unripe, or rotten, as he reached his hands gingerly along the simulacra of branches. He eased his hunger a little.

But the light waves lagged more than a season. The slender trunk he saw had, to his hands, a huge girth. He could not reach round the massive unseen girth: yet he could readily have clasped his arms around the slender stem he saw. When he tried to do so, of course, the unseen girth prevented him, grazing his knuckles when he incautiously reached out. He brooded on the disparity. A tree with such a girth might be two hundred years old: the one he saw before him might be less than twenty.

He could not judge accurately. He took the figure two hundred for convenience, for an arbitrary certainty within the confusion. But it might have been three hundred; it might have been three thousand years. How long did it take the light of the most distant stars to reach the earth, the light of stars already exploded? And at his analogy he suddenly sickened, that he saw around him the light waves of a dead village, villagers perhaps centuries dead manifest before him through some physical aberration.

Slowly, through the day of his illumination, realization spread. He might never escape the valley: if anyone came looking for him, on foot, by air, he would not see them, nor they him, unless they could see into the future the slow travelling images of the present; and no one could. He might hear searchers, for sound waves seemed as he had always known them; but he could not shout constantly to attract them who might never come: he could not light fires of sound like the castaway's smoke signal. He thought, momentarily, that perhaps he could: ignite the whole valley, and the sound of its blazing and crackling might be heard: but the flames would be sightless, so that he would never be able to avoid them, would be burnt unwittingly, by invisible fire. And he could not find his way from the valley for he could never know its geography, its vegetation: he could use his eyes only with the sort of credence he would give to ancient charts and obsolete maps, without even knowing their possible antiquity. Earthquake, landslide, erosion, flooding, the shifting, changing, burgeoning of vegetation were not recorded for him, had all changed.

VIII

He grew weaker, unable to find sufficient fruit, unable to find other food. The villagers passed through and around him, and they grew familiar to him, in one way more familiar that they were to each other whom they never saw. But they spoke to each other and he never heard them. And they never knew him. As he grew weaker, and perhaps delirious, he wondered if the girl, in whose room he sat each night, watching hopelessly over her nakedness which he tried and always failed to touch, perhaps had dreamed of him two hundred, two thousand, years ago. He imagined that her smiles, as she slept, were smiles of her dreaming with longing of him, as he now longed for her. In desperation he would lie beside her, his invisibility beside her full visible nakedness, his tactile palpability beside her wraith-like emptiness. He spent each night beside her, watching her, calling her, weeping for her to respond. But she had died two hundred, two thousand, years before. And how would she have imagined him in her dreams, she who had seen no man, unless the ghosts of her ancestors?

And sometimes he would wonder, half with terror, half with futile curiosity, who might be there, in two hundred, two thousand, years' time ahead, to watch his hopeless love for an object then no longer visible, his slow death creeping on him now, the final disintegration and decay invisible till then.

THE WONDERFULLY INTELLIGENT SHEEP-DOG

Dal Stivens

By rights the wind ought to have been using my whitened ribs as a xylophone weeks ago and the crows ought to have been as fat as ticks from feeding on my unattended mob of sheep, with me tossed in as a before-dinner titbit. I was in the back of the outback, two hundred miles from anywhere, with a broken leg; but instead of having to risk a knock on the Pearly Gates everything was dodger. My leg was healing as well as it would in one of those posh city hospitals, my mob was thriving and growing pound notes right under my eyes, and the crows were too scared of Peggy, my kelpie sheep-dog, to poke their noses out of the gorge where she'd chased them.

To make things even more snitcher I was living on the fat of the land, and in a few minutes I'd sit down to a plate of roast wild duck that would have set me back ten bob at one of those flash Sydney restaurants. About an hour ago a mob of black ducks had come soaring past and settled on the billabong.

"By gosh, I'd like to sink my molars into one of those," I said aloud to myself. I'd got into the habit long ago.

I'd hardly finished talking before Peggy, my kelpie sheep-bitch, was tugging the Cashmore out of the back of the sulky. She lugs it over to where I lay in my camp stretcher and then went off to fetch me some cartridges. I couldn't see the point of it though, because the billabong was a good quarter of a mile away and there's no shot gun made that will carry that far.

I should have trusted the kelpie. All kelpies are beautiful with sheep and as intelligent as you like. But none I ever struck were in the same paddock as Peggy. She pelted off towards that billabong and scared the blackies into the air. I expected them to head away, but Peggy knew what she was doing. There was a mirage just by my camp and, just as Peggy had worked it out, they took it for water and settled on the ground. I let them have both barrels and bagged seventeen.

If Peggy had had fingers she'd have plucked and cleaned them there and then, but she did almost everything else while I fixed the ducks up. She dragged fresh wood onto the fire, brought the pan to me, and fetched the fat tin.

I'd done my leg in six weeks ago. I went head over turkey out of the sulky when the right wheel hit a log I hadn't seen.

"Well," I told myself then. "You'll do a perish, mate, and no mistake. You're two hundred miles as the crow flies from anywhere."

Talking of crows, there were millions of 'em and as soon as they saw me lying on the ground, they came and perched in the trees right over my head, cawing loudly, and sharpening their beaks on the branches, and telling themselves that supper wouldn't be long. But as it turned out they reckoned without Peggy.

I lay on the ground and thought it over. It was queer country where I was, and I could believe that no one else had ever been here except perhaps an odd swaggie like the bloke who had told me about this valley. Six months earlier the big drought had made me take to the roads with my mob of a thousand sheep. Others were in the long paddock like myself and there weren't many pickings for my mob, which were losing condition fast. Then the swaggie I'd helped out with some tobacco put me on to this spot. It was only five days' going from where I was, but it turned out to be tough. I lost a couple of hundred ewes and two of three dogs got sick and turned up their toes, leaving me only Peggy. For the last three days I had to head across country too hungry to support a cockroach. I wondered why the hell I had ever listened to that sundowner. But when we got through the valley mouth everything was dodger. The grass was thick, up to the sulky's floor in places, and there was plenty of water. Here was rich ten-pound-an-acre country in the middle of a stretch you wouldn't give tenpence an acre for — and I had it to myself. And then I had to do my leg in.

So many crows had perched in the big gums around me that their limbs began to droop like weeping willows.

"Well, I suppose I'd better try some splints," I said aloud to myself. The next thing Peggy is beating it off into the bush and although I yelled and whistled to her to come back, she took no notice. It wasn't like her and I put it down to the queer something or other I felt about this stretch of country. It wasn't natural, for one thing, for there to be so many crows. When I thought Peggy had cleared out I felt pretty low, I can tell you. But in less time than it takes to tell you this, Peggy is back with two bits of bark she has gnawed off, which are just the right length for splints. Before I'd quite cottoned on to what I had to do with them, Peggy has raced off again and is scrounging round the back of the sulky for an old shirt I had stowed there for me to tear into bandages.

While I'm doing that Peggy cuts loose on the crows. I've heard blokes claim the kelpies they owned were so smart they could work flies into the neck of a beer bottle, but they had nothing on Peggy. Almost before I've fixed the splints Peggy has worked those kellies into a single mob and taken the black death birds a mile up the valley where she yards them into a gorge and leaves them there, cawing madly but not game to move out. Peggy comes pelting back just as I'm saying, "I'd have a chance now if I could get the tent fixed up. That and a good meal would help."

The words are hardly out before Peggy is tearing around looking for poles for the tent. She had some trouble biting through the young saplings, but in the end we had enough, and we got the tent rigged between us, though Peggy had hardly enough weight for laying back on the ropes.

When the tent was up and I'd crawled into the camp stretcher I started thinking how hungry I was and was just about to tell Peggy to fetch me the hunk of corn beef; but she had other ideas. She reckoned I needed some fresh meat now that I was an invalid, and scooted away into the bush. In about ten minutes she came back with a three-quarters grown buck which I skinned and cut up. I'd barely finished the job before she was waving a bit of bark under my nose and making signs for me to put a match to it, and in no time she had built a good roasting fire.

I lived for about a month on rabbits and wild pigeons which Peggy used to stalk and catch, and then I felt like a change of diet, particularly when I saw that mob of black ducks. Well, as I told you, Peggy worked the mirage lurk on them, and did those blackies taste good!

Peggy didn't stop at roast duck, however. I noticed that evening that she seemed upset about something. She started walking round and round in circles and every now and then she'd sigh and put a paw behind her ear.

Then suddenly she barked excitedly and beat it off into the bush and came back with Blossom, my sulky mare. While I was wondering what she was up to, she scoots off again and comes back, dragging a largish tree branch with her. She made signs to me and after a bit I cottoned on to what she wanted and hitched Blossom to the branch. As soon as that was done, Peggy chases Blossom up to the billabong and into the water. Blossom doesn't want to go in at first but Peggy isn't in a mood for any nonsense. She drives Blossom up and down and back and across that billabong. The water gets muddy and fish start choking and begin floating to the top, belly upwards. Peggy fetches in two big Murray cod and a catfish. She must have forgotten I didn't like catfish.

Afterwards, I'd only got to say I'd like some fish and Blossom would head for the bush; but, of course, she never got very far before Peggy brought her back for me to hitch to a tree branch. A couple of times Peggy varied the menu by diving into the billabong and working a couple of hundred crays into a kerosene tin she'd set on the bank. She knew I was partial to yabbies. Peggy, by the way, was well in pup by this time, but she stuck to her job.

Just about this time, I noticed something queer was happening to the sheep. I thought I was going nuts at first. The sheep were growing green wool. And Blossom was growing green hair. When I got over the shock I worked it out it must be something to do with the grass and it being spring because Peggy still kept her usual red colour. So each day for a week I nibbled a handful of the grass and sure enough my own hair and beard began to turn green. It grew so quick too that it was down to my knees in a couple of days. I knocked off eating the grass then, of course, because green wasn't a colour I'd choose myself for my hair or beard. As soon as I stopped eating the grass my hair went back to its usual brown.

The trouble with Blossom was, the green hair grew so fast that she stumbled over her mane and she could scarcely see. I had to clip her every three days and at first it was something to keep me occupied, but after a while I got fed up, particularly when I had to do it every second day.

I was worried now about the sheep because their green wool was soon about ten feet long and they couldn't move without treading on each other's fleeces and tripping each other up. They were blind as bats, too, and couldn't find their way to drink at the billabong without Peggy helping them there.

To make things worse Peggy was just about to drop her pups and this slowed her up in her work. Three of them arrived one night and before their eyes were open Peggy started training them to work the sheep. The pups made a bit of difference when they grew up a little, but I could see the job was getting too big. The fleeces were now twenty feet long and I had to clip Blossom every day. The sheep were falling over every few minutes.

"I wish there was some way of shearing the sheep," I

said to myself.

Before I can blink Peggy is heading for the billabong and barking for the three pups, all bitches, to follow her. All four kelpies dive into the water and I heard a great deal of barking and splashing going on. In about five minutes I noticed a great black and grey mass crawling over the ground. It's like a wave, about four feet high, and when it gets near I see that Peggy and her pups have hunted millions and millions of crayfish out of the billabong. Before I can tumble to what it is all about, the yabbies are crawling all over the sheep and nipping off the fleeces. You wouldn't credit how quickly those crays shore the sheep, only, of course, there were so many of them. Soon there were fleeces all over the place.

"You're a smart girl, Peggy," I told her, "but the fleeces ought to be gathered up."

Peggy just barked at me as though to let me know there was nothing to worry about because she's worked out a way of fixing that, too. And she had, by golly. I hadn't noticed before, but the fleeces were getting stacked together. Peggy had her pups yarding up the bulldog and meat ants to do the job. My eyes were sticking out like organ-stops by the time the ants had finished, because they heaped all that lovely green wool into a stack as high as a six-story building.

I was still marvelling at all this when I heard Blossom squealing her head off and saw that Peggy had sooled some of the crays on to clipping her hair. That pleased me nearly as much as all that beautiful wool that was already dyed.

It got into summer and the sheep started growing yellow wool. Almost all the ewes had lambed in the spring and the lambs grew yellow wool, too, just as fast as their mothers. Occasionally a few of the crows sneaked out of the gorge and tried to peck some of the wool out of the sheep's backs, but Peggy stopped their caper pretty smartly and hunted them back. I was able to get about now, but had to leave the work to Peggy and her pups, of course. I wouldn't have known how to start making the yabbies do their job. It was pretty hot, so Peggy sooled the crays on to the shearing every ten or twelve days. By the end of summer I had a great stack of yellow wool, a little bigger, if anything, than that of the green wool. It was as good as growing five-pound notes.

I kept tag of the days on a calendar a storekeeper had given me and one day when I was crossing off a day Peggy took a peek over my shoulder and suddenly got so excited, barking and jumping up, that I had to chase her away. What had got her worked up was the coloured picture of a Highlander in the Campbell of Breadalbane tartan on the calendar, and I put it down to her having got a kick in the ribs from a bloke in kilts at a Highland gathering on New Year's Day — or perhaps it was Peggy's Scottish blood coming out. Kelpies were bred from smooth-haired Scotch collies of the black-and-tan variety with possibly a bit of dingo, as you know, and are the most wonderfully intelligent sheep-dogs in the world.

When we started running into autumn I wondered what coloured wool the sheep would grow next. Don't ask me why, but it turned out to be blue, and by and by I had a large heap of blue wool.

I kept ticking the days off the calendar, and as winter came along the sheep began to grow black wool. About this time Peggy and her pups ran into a spot of trouble with the crays. Most days now they took a bit of driving to their work and would try to sneak off into the bush. I can't say I blamed them, because their claws were getting worn down with all the nipping they had to do.

"We won't be able to work the poor yabbies much longer," I said. "We'll never be able to shear this black wool."

Peggy just barked as though to say she thought I was a damn fool. It struck me then she had been cheeky on a number of occasions lately. But I let it pass. Peggy tore up the valley. I wasn't left long wondering what she and the pups were up to. In a few minutes there's such a cawing and croaking that it made my ears shake. Then about three million crows burst overhead in formation and went to work pecking the wool out of the sheep. If anything they were quicker than the yabbies, and I wondered then why Peggy hadn't used the kellies before. But she was right as usual. Each time they pecked the wool out during the next few weeks they pinched some of it for their nests, and the black heap, as it turned out, wasn't as tall as I had expected. All the same, it was a fair stack and I had no complaints.

"There's a fortune for me with all this wool," I said, looking at the four heaps. "It's a pity it couldn't be woven on the spot. It's already dyed but it needs scouring."

Hardly had I said this before Peggy and her three pups are beating it off into the bush. They are gone about an hour and I'm wondering what they can be up to when I see a couple of hundred whirlwinds twisting and turning up the mouth of the valley. They make a roar like thunder as they pass my camp, and I have to jam my fingers in my ears. I can hardly believe what I'm seeing, but Peggy and her pups are working those willy-willies and driving them where they want them. In the next few minutes so much happens that I wonder if my eyes are letting me down. First the whirlwinds are worked into the big heaps of coloured wool and the wool is caught up and goes swirling and twisting into the air. With a roar like a thousand express trains crossing a thousand overhead bridges together the wool is whisked through the billabong and comes out scoured. With a roar like a billion stock-whips all cracking together it is whirled up into the sky and spun into yarn. First, the heap of green wool, and then the others, in turn, are twirled so high and so fast your eyes can hardly follow. I've never seen any kelpies work more beautifully than Peggy and her pups did with those willy-willies.

In the next hour the sky is so full of wool being spun and then woven it is like looking at a giant maypole or about a dozen Auroras-Australis. These willy-willies went leaping and bouncing across the sky so fast I got dizzy and gave up trying to work out what they were up to, and sat back in my stretcher for a rest. They were half-way through their work before I woke up to what was happening to the wool. I was so surprised I fell out of the stretcher and got a lump on the back of my head. It's still there if you care to have a look. Those willy-willies had woven all that coloured wool into a huge piece of Campbell of Breadalbane tartan — green ground with black and blue half-inch crossings and a double yellow overcheck — four miles wide and already about seven miles long, stretching up into the sky, and only half finished.

I thought it was just a fluke at first, and then I remembered how excited Peggy had been that day when she peeked over my shoulder and saw the Highlander on the calendar.

With all that tartan material I was a made man, though, it is true, I had a bit of trouble getting it out before I finished. Peggy had to rope the yabbies in to cut that great piece of Campbell tartan into lengths, and they nearly jibbed on it. They had got a bit wild while the crows had been on the job, but in the end they did what Peggy wanted.

I had to get three hundred and twenty-seven bullock-teams to cart the lengths to the city. Peggy had some idea of making the crows do the job, but a bloke would have looked a bit silly following a lot of kellies along George Street, Sydney.

LET IT RING

John Foyster

3.2 Gray lay the land, oh, says the old poet. It hardly seems so now. Even then it was an illusion, but now our illusions are so much better prepared. Our isolation for example.

If we were rich only in illusion it would not matter, this time. How sad that we are actually rich! It is so much more difficult to die.

Is it becoming more difficult to keep this up, or is it just the concern with the events to come? More time would help. But there is none.

The one about the 3-legged dwarf, for L.

In: 746
Out: 428   Only modest.

Drank too much again. Must be more abstemious.

Plans: To convince the Council to act correctly will need more than I alone can achieve, but at the same time the required action is so careful a balance that inducing others to work will increase the chance of error, and the slightest error is not permissible. Only Kenners really

120

knows what I want, and even he suspects my intent. So that is the first barrier to be removed; but it must be done without artifice, or the attempt will have been wasted.

Two — no amount of speaking can convince *them*. Only here on Strine are words effective, and even then (I should know) things go slowly, and that is precisely the point, old friend. I am sure we have much to offer, and much to gain: these must be maximized, and I can't afford to be too scrupulous.

This seems a damned silly business, almost all of the time, but since there have occasionally been advantages in the past I suppose the habit is worth continuing.

Strine to *gain:* firmer contact, faster access, development potential.

Federation to *gain:* cultural enrichment (slight), market of sorts (again slight). No, it is all on our side, *provided that we do not become a bound colony.* Few have won that game: we must be exceptional. And the margin for error so *small* !

If Kenners, then possibly Mathers also. They are close, but I must move stealthily — that's too strong a word to be used in first person like this, but that's how it must seem, but to no one.

K

and then

M

A celebration? Yes, but *not* a wake!

ACTION!

ACTION! I said. Get that thing mov — ah, that's real nice . . !

Commissioner Turners strolled gaily across the pebbled path that was his in trust. No need to loiter, this fine day. Work, yes, work, would solve all the problems.

CUT!

Oh balls, how many times, how *many* times — this old futz is *old* — OH-EL-DEE. He moves *slowly.* Slowly!

3.3 Time is burning and the world on fire, said the poet. It almost seems as though he knew. Certainly a decision is close, and now even five days almost singes the heels. If tomorrow is as today was . . . Ah, but each day I *must* learn something. I think Kenners appreciates my position, but he is so hesitant. Certainly he has a great deal to lose, but I have more, and for Strine it is everything — and so no sleep tonight.

Simple points: almost everyone wants in, but few seem to be able to remember the past. Odd, with so much information available, that it should be regarded as sacrilegious to examine that which is common to us all, and to be concerned with the trivial present. We want in, but on our terms. Too many don't care about those terms. Take —— for example — no concern for the past at all. Consequence — no future, except a secure slavery. Every physical thing sold for one heart's desires. That is too easy a path, and that is its popularity. No point in proposing this: only the advantages of alternatives.

K sees all this *I am sure.* He distrusts me, for I, an isolate man, am suddenly become gregarious. But this models our world's situation. Yes, I must put it to him in this way. He appreciates that sort of approach — men as islands, seas of troubles and so on.

Out: 47 Not Today.

The enthusiasm of all was somewhat lessened today, I would guess, and this would be favourable, or will be in five day's time. If the mood were only to continue pessimistic for a few days more — say until 5, perhaps 6. Thus by 8 my approach will not only be welcomed by those who know me, but by those who are now (and will then be) vacillating. What now is dark would then be light. But how to keep things going down? And then to recover?

To be associated with the Welkin is essential to our

future, this I know: but it seems that we can move only partly on our own terms. And suppose that *their* strength should become ours? Now *there* is an angle to be exploited! To use and be used may be even more difficult, but the reward is high. But that is for the future: the present is close enough — too close.

Must be particularly skilled at the game tomorrow — to lose face now would be disastrous.

X, but hardly worthwhile.

An old man huddled, scratching. CU back. The man stretches one arm, rubs his hands together, and resumes writing.

If it is possible to draw M into my conversation with K — that would be the best approach — but not until K is already hooked; though perhaps when he is struggling with the focus of the argument? Hard to say. Either if he is raising silly objections or is almost convinced, either will do. Late in the afternoon, at that.

Sell! That will do it! A simple manipulation, which will have to be carefully controlled, but it *can* be controlled. Only low wagers — that will help too.

Incomplete — I could never understand the importance anyway —

3.4 Luck is hot and people funny. If only it could be joked about! K's attitude is inexplicable, unless someone else is getting to him. Or perhaps the Federation is paying him off? Whatever the cause, my attempts were so unsuccessful that all must be changed. Of course Mathers was surprisingly helpful towards the end of that rather painful conversation, and perhaps he can be counted on, but that isn't enough. And he may be playing a double game.

Otherwise a successful day. Sales went well, and money is sliding, though slowly, on all sides. Down three per cent, which is large enough to be rattling, but not serious. Game smooth, though lacking in energy.

3.5 Tell me what your heart has hidden, says the poet. Well, I shall certainly have to do that — not easy, but necessary. Oh, on the last day In 426, Out 357, today In 433, Out 439. Necessary to consider what roll 'em to play.

My Dear Kenners:

I feel that I may have expressed myself either inelegantly or inexactly at our meeting yesterday, and hasten to take this opportunity to describe my position with greater clarity. First let me note that I regard the subject of our conversation and of this letter as of the greatest importance — I could hardly do otherwise — and feel that the too-readily-grasping attitude of some commissioners, responsive as it is to the great inducements offered to us, yet overlooks some of the dangers inherent in a sudden *surrender*. Perhaps you feel this last word is too strong, and I am inclined to think that it was partly a result of my crude expression of this feeling of mine in our conversation yesterday which led to the conclusion which was, to my mind, unsatisfactory. While the treasures of a galaxy may be offered to us, I think it unwise to forget that we have to pay a price of some kind: it is the fact that this price has not been spelled out in detail which most worries me.

Perhaps if I outline my understanding of our present situation in some detail you will find it easier to come to the conclusion which I assumed in outlining my plan to you. You were affronted then, but perhaps you will come to appreciate my concern and thus what appears now as ruthlessness.

We know from our limited contact with the Federation that Strine is a small but comparatively rich world. The Galactic Federation is, by contrast, very large, and comparatively poor. Comparatively, because there are many poor worlds in the Federation, as well as the few rich ones. When our commissioners think of the Federation, they think of the rich worlds, and forget the poor. I try to think of the poor — in the physical sense. But to return to the point. I know that it is now unfashionable to invoke the name of the Blessed Father Damien, but his warnings from the past seem almost directed to this hour. In his *Speculative History* the Holy One writes of empires:

"Only the insane attempt to seize power: only the strong maintain it. Beware, therefore, the powerful revolutionary."

(A warning to us all, perhaps, but later he continues:)

"Under the circumstances, any attempt to establish interstellar hegemony (much less a galactic empire) must be regarded in one of two ways: as a manifestation of insanity, in the context previously discussed, or as a drive for power of the paranoid type. This latter, in the past, has led to ephemeral (on the large scale) ultra-authoritarian regimes of unspeakable cruelty."

Now we do not know *enough* about this "Galactic Federation". We know that it *seems* benevolent. We know that membership *seems* to be by invitation, and that some worlds are known to have refused. But we cannot experience for ourselves being a part of this Federation. And no world has ever *left* the Federation, a circumstance open to at least two interpretations. I am prepared to accept that the Federation is indeed benevolent, and that on this occasion the Blessed Father Damien's foresight was at fault. But I do not believe that we can realistically approach this union in the lighthearted way espoused by some of our fellows: we must beware of the dangers, and we must remember that these will not be immediately apparent.

Now our situation is this: though we are committed to enter the Federation we can still, in fact, opt out (though there are very few persons of influence here on Strine who would even consider such a proposition, more's the pity). Such an action would set back our full admission to the Federation decades — perhaps even longer — and for this reason, if no other, such an action could only be taken after careful and dispassionate, I repeat *dispassionate*, study of the function of the Federation as it now is. That is the first problem: to make our fellows (you see, I am already accounting you as one of my associates) realize that this is a practical, not a theoretical, course of action. When this has been established, and only then, we can move on to the more serious problem. Almost all of us are now determined, I think, to try for the right to host a Welkin, that festival of worlds at which, according to our lights, we can measure the extents of co-operation and coercion between the various worlds of the Federation. We cannot possibly offer for any of the next four or five Welkins, but we will of course send delegations to those to spy out the land. Those who are opposed to us see this as an opportunity for sporting and fun: I, and you I trust, see it as, regrettably, a matter of some seriousness, though I must confess that my age has somewhat lessened my enthusiasm for the more popular sports.

And there is that other, most serious of problems. In my mind it is essential that we should, before finally joining the Federation, examine the broad *and* the specific reactions of those of the Federation to our own beautiful world. I will emphasize it: those of the Federation. It is presently supposed that, as a result of the clamour of so many new worlds to join the Federation, and the desire of each and every one to host a Welkin (in the main, I would suppose, for reasons much the same as ours), Welkins should be held on non-Federation worlds far more than has been the case in the past. Many have looked on this suggestion with favour, including many of our own commissioners. I, as you know, oppose the idea: not so much because it is my nature (and you know that such is *not* my nature), but because it will deprive us of that vital test we need. For I believe, and I think you agree with me, that as the Welkin moves further from the Federation, so will the interest of the Federation decline. Perhaps slowly at first, but inevitably. Since we are committed, except under the circumstances I have suggested above, which are dismissed as "impossible" by so many of our colleagues, to a course of action leading inevitably to our absorption into the Federation we must measure the Federation: if we hope to do so by hosting a Welkin we need the Federation to be present, dominant. And it is my immovable belief that if more non-Federation planets host Welkins then within a few years, by the time that we on Strine are ready for our turn, so few Federation representatives will be present that our measures will be illusory: the Welkin will be dominated by non-Federation worlds wanting tips for the future. It is for these, and perhaps other, reasons that I propose to speak on Nine, and I hope that I will have your support and that of others.

Believe me to be your sincere friend,
Ring the bells and climb the steeple
Turners
going
to screw the people.

I think that puts across the main points. At least K will be prepared for the events of three days hence.

Sales still dropping, but the prices are bottoming. In 339, Out 448. Aie! for me.

3.6 The wheels of fate are spinning around. How appropriate are the words of the old poet! For my letter cannot help but be regarded as a foolish thing. Though the gain may be great, the striving was not proportionate. What was gained with Mathers, today, so joyfully, may have been lost irretrievably by that over-anxious letter. Were I younger I should not have made such a mistake: indeed, I think I must have had the opportunity to make mistakes of such a magnitude in the past, and my writing these quiet words now is a tribute to my youthful caution. Soon I may have no such fond memories of the past. There are times when a son — but no, abhorrent thought!

Nevertheless, prices have flattened completely, with minor oscillations. Sales still drop, but this is favourable, today. Tomorrow there must be a slight upward turn. I feel that it will not take a great investment to introduce the necessary optimism. Shall I guess a figure? No, with my difficulties such a game is, well, a game. If *only* I had not sent K so detailed a letter! Nowhere do I make myself so explicit that it is dangerous, but to have been so hasty, with so much at stake, and with so little to gain. 325-146.

FADE TO: puzzled face.
Cut to CU diarist's back.

3.7 Tell me, love, what you most desire! Ah, Anthony, this would have been a day for you! No more glorious day can I remember, even far, far in the days when I, a springing, jounced my way over those goddamn pebbles. Those pebbles! Ah, the rough with the smooth, and now?

3.75 Ever? One, sales recovered slightly. Two, prices excellent. Three, the replies of Kenners, both oral and written, are almost too encouraging. Though a great weight has been lifted (and indeed, while Kenners is now occupying my gloomy estate of yesterday) there is much to be done. Mathers must be won over more completely, *necessarily* alone. Not easy, for him or me. A risk.

I am beginning (at my age) to see why the custom is as it is. By consulting these notes, more closely than I have ever done before, I can not only come to understand my own frailty and changeability, but there are almost moments when the changes are predictable. Learning from the past mistake is one thing: having a half-perception of the future, though dangerous, can be well-used to great advantage.

Nil. (Of course.)
Now, it seems, the numbers are safe. But we are not yet safe. A little greater effort — that is all.

3.8

Sirs and Masters,

I am known to you all as a simple and humble man. In bringing forward these few simple and humble thoughts I am not only aware that to most of you what I have to say will be a little too obvious, and the minds of those others will only be examining these artless and superficial notions for profundities they do not contain.

I come before the Council simply and humbly, as is my wont, but I believe that in some way I can represent to you views which are not merely my straightforward observations, but which also are common amongst the citizens of this our world. It is thus humbly I come forward, yet proudly that I hope to speak for my people.

Sirs and Masters:

As all organisms grow or die so, it seems, do worlds. It is for this reason (and for others with which I shall not trouble you) that the High Council in its wisdom has decided to establish a beach-head for growth: to associate the planet Strine with the Galactic Federation, that organization of worlds whose brief contacts with us have already brought to us so many wonders and benefits. Not only is the Federation large and rich: it is wise. The Federation realizes that young worlds (and our own is young, in some ways) having a First Contact face severe problems. Thus the Federation says to the newly-discovered worlds: join us if you will. There is no hurry. Do so at your own pace. Even after you have committed yourself to joining us, you may withdraw at any stage up to the final signing without any feeling from us. And we will provide technological advances of many kinds for your own development, whether you decide to join us or not.

Sirs and Masters:

The Federation is like, if I may return us all to the past we have nearly forgotten, a fairy godmother: something we

129

might long for, and then be surprised to discover as actually existing. We have decided, as obviously we should, that to join the Federation will make way for great development of Strine. Thus far, of course, we are only in preliminary stages: investigating, as it were. For the Federation, in its wisdom, advises and even encourages new planets to travel through the Federation observing the machine in motion, and, if I may say this without offence, the oiling of its cogs. As our saying has it, crack the nakful shell and remain a vegetarian.

All this the Federation does, for all new worlds. There are some few of us, I understand, who approach this matter lightheartedly, as well we all might, for it is a joyous thing to discover that one's childhood dreams are true. But there are others, like myself, who feel that the great honour we have been offered should be treated with great seriousness, as being a matter of the greatest importance and therefore deserving of the most careful scrutiny. We are all men who appreciate the good things of life, but there is not one of us who has not come by them by sweat. There is not one of us who comes to this place who is not scrupulously careful in all the details of personal business. There is not one of us who would give his house to a stranger. And there is not one of us here who would trust him who gives away all that he has for a promise.

Sirs and Masters:

I am speaking plainly, for I am a simple man. The Federation will not honour us for treating their offer lightly. Like greedy schoolchildren to gobble all that is offered without thought. Sirs, we *honour* the Federation by closely examining it before our own final commitment.

Thus I am greatly pleased that we have chosen to not only send our ambassadors to far worlds to discern their nature, but also to invite men from all worlds of the Federation to visit ours, so that we may see their reactions to our strangeness.

But sirs, I ask of you this: are we concerned with the reactions of members of the Federation, or with the reactions of all off-worldlings? For me there can be but one answer. Though we must observe all, our interest, in this matter, must be confined to those who will most influence our future: so far as we know, to members of the Federation: citizens of planets such as we shall become.

And how is all this to come about? Each four hundred standard days a great symposium is held, and has been held for hundreds of years (our time), at which gather the people of the entire galaxy, from both Federation and non-Federation planets. Far in the past, these Welkins were held only on Federation planets, and thus were a showpiece for the Federation. Now this is not so, for since the time of the Tornto Welkin, many of these gatherings have been held on non-Federation worlds. I expect the motivation for those worlds has been much the same as our own: to examine the stranger on familiar ground. Until our own time relatively few Welkins have been held on non-Federation worlds. But now things may be changed.

Sirs and Masters:

The enthusiasm of non-Federation worlds for an increased opportunity of having the honour of staging a Welkin can be well understood. We feel it ourselves. But who of us can predict the consequence of change? And who of us has such great faith in that power of prediction? Is not our whole way of life based upon the assumption of certainty?

Sirs and Masters:

I have heard the views of those who say — let us share in this greater wealth. I have been encouraged by my own observations of life in the Federation. I am greatly encouraged and wholly optimistic.

But sirs, to treat the Federation and its offer lightheartedly is to treat it with contempt. We should not take up a part of this grand offer: we should accept the whole, and steadfastly pursue our thorough investigation of the Federation's workings.

And this has been threatened. Not deliberately, but almost unthinkingly. To be sure, there are many worlds in the galaxy. To be sure, many of them seek membership of the Federation. But the best resolution of this happy and unhappy situation is not to hawk the Welkin to every jumped-up planetoid. The best resolution is not to despatch the Welkin to the furthest arms of the galaxy. For to do this is to destroy the Welkin as we know it, *and as we wish to use it ourselves.* For soon after these proposed changes we should find decreasing numbers of Federation members visiting the sites of this once-great event. The expansion, and the time of preparation involved, will force Federation members to lose interest in what was once their glory.

I do not ask that you accept everything I suggest, true though it is. All I have asked and am now asking is this: that we should treat this matter as one of great moment, as it deserves, and that we should present at the next Welkin the views I have here presented for further discussion.

I am your servant, Lords.

That should, at least with some amplification, swing enough of them: how fortunate it is that the importance of presenting an argument weakly is not widely understood! Sometimes age is an advantage. On all other sides the result is success. I am content, now. Prices starting to rally nicely. All will be well, I am sure.

3.9 The challenge holds, I cannot now retract.
The boast I made to that relentless court.

Now I can only wait: the reaction seemed right, and the coin clinked ringingly. They cannot reject me out of hand. They cannot ignore me, either. But again I am uncertain, and I did not expect to feel that emotion *now*.

3.10 Is there anybody here or is everybody dead? asked

the poet, as I ask now, I am too old to care. Should I not have left them? I will not be here. A childish fantasy cannot do harm to children. But to their children. Tomorrow I shall know, as we all will.

3.11 Yes.
FADE
"Hey honey," she said, "what about the Nazhfiki?" heels drummed urgently.
"I haven't tried . . ."
Roll 'em roll 'em roll 'em
ROLL 'EM ROLL 'EM ROLL 'EM

THE
MOUNTAIN MOVERS

A. Bertram Chandler

Olgana — Earth-type, revolving around a Sol-type primary — is a backwater planet. It is well off the main Galactic trade routes, although it gets by quite comfortably by exporting meat, butter, wool and the like to the neighbouring, highly industrialised Mekanika System. Olgana was a Lost Colony, one of those worlds stumbled upon quite by chance during the First Expansion, settled in a spirit of great thankfulness by the personnel of a hopelessly off course, completely lost emigrant lodejammer. It was rediscovered — this time with no element of chance involved — by the survey Service's *Trail Blazer*, before the colonists had drifted too far from the mainstream of human culture. Shortly thereafter there were legal proceedings against these same colonists, occupying a few argumentative weeks at the Federation's Court of Galactic Justice in Geneva, on Earth; had these been successful they would have been followed by an Eviction Order. Even in those days it was illegal for humans to establish themselves on any planet already supporting an intelligent life form. *But* — and the colonists' Learned Counsel made the most of it — that law had not been in existence when *Lode Jumbuk* lifted off from Port Woomera on what turned out to be her last voyage. It was only a legal quibble, but the aborigines had no representation at Court — and, furthermore, Counsel for the Defense had hinted, in the right quarters, that if he lost his case he would bring suit on behalf of his clients against the Interstellar Transport Commission, holding that body fully responsible for the plight of *Lode Jumbuk*'s castaways and their descendants. ITC, fearing that a dangerous and expensive precedent might be established, brought behind-the-scenes pressure to bear and the case was dropped. Nobody asked the aborigines what they thought about it all.

There was no denying that the Olganan natives — if they were natives — were a backward race. They were humanoid — to outward appearances human. They did not, however, quite fit into the general biological pattern of their world, the fauna of which mainly comprised very primitive egg-laying mammals. The aborigines were mammals as highly developed as Man himself, although along slightly different lines. There had been surprisingly little research into Olganan biology, however; the Colony's highly competent biologists seemed to be entirely lacking in the spirit of scientific curiosity. They were biological engineers rather than scientists, their main concern being to improve the strains of their meat-producing and wool-bearing animals, descended in the main from the spermatozoa and ova which *Lode Jumbuk* — as did all colonization vessels of her period — had carried under refrigeration.

To Olgana came the Survey Service's Serpent Class Courier *Adder*, Lieutenant John Grimes commanding. She carried not-very-important despatches for Commander Lewin, Officer-in-Charge of the small Federation Survey Service Base maintained on the planet. The despatches were delivered and then, after the almost mandatory small talk, Grimes asked, "And would there be any Orders for me, Commander?"

Lewin — a small, dark, usually intense man — grinned. "Of a sort, Lieutenant. Of a sort. You must be in Commodore Damien's good books. When *I* was skipper of a Courier it was always a case of getting from Point A to Point B as soon as possible, if not before, with stopovers

135

cut down to the irreducible minimum . . . Well, since you ask, I received a Carlottigram from Officer Commanding Couriers just before you blew in. I am to inform you that there will be no employment for your vessel for a period of at least six weeks local. You and your officers are to put yourselves at my disposal . . . " The Commander grinned again. "I find it hard enough to find jobs enough to keep my own personnel as much as half busy. So . . . enjoy yourselves. Go your merry ways rejoicing, as long as you carry your personal transceivers at all times. See the sights, such as they are. Wallow in the fleshpots — such as *they* are." He paused. "I only wish that the Commodore had loved me as much as he seems to love you."

"Mphm," grunted Grimes, his prominent ears reddening. "I don't think that it's quite that way, sir." He was remembering his last interview with Damien. *Get out of my sight!* the Commodore had snarled. *Get out of my sight, and don't come back until I'm in a better temper if ever . . .*

"Indeed?" with a sardonic lift of the eyebrows.

"It's this way, Commander. I don't think that I'm overly popular around Lindisfarn Base at the moment . . . "

Lewin laughed outright. "I'd guessed as much. Your fame, Lieutenant, has spread even to Olgana. Frankly, I don't want you in *my* hair, around *my* Base, humble though it be. The administration of this planet is none of my concern, luckily, so you and your officers can carouse to your hearts' content as long as it's not in *my* bailiwick."

"Have you any suggestions, sir?" asked Grimes stiffly.

"Why, yes. There's the so-called Gold Coast. It got started after the Trans-Galactic Clippers started calling here on their cruises."

"Inflated prices," grumbled Grimes. "A tourist trap . . . "

"How right you are. But not every TG cruise passenger is a millionaire. I could recommend, perhaps, the coach tour of Nevernever. You probably saw it from Space on

136

your way in — that whacking great island continent in the Southern Hemisphere."

"How did it get its name?"

"The natives call it that — or something that sounds almost like that. It's the only continent upon which the aborigines live, by the way. When *Lode Jumbuk* made her landing there was no intelligent life at all in the Northern Hemisphere."

"What's so attractive about this tour?"

"Nevernever is the only unspoiled hunk of real estate on the planet. It has been settled along the coastal fringe by humans, but the Outback — which means the Inland and most of the country north of Capricorn — is practically still the way it was when Men first came here. Oh, there're sheep and cattle stations, and a bit of mining, but there won't be any real development, with irrigation and all the rest, until population pressure forces it. And the aborigines — well, most of them — still live in the semi-desert the way they did before *Lode Jumbuk* came." Lewin was warming up. "Think of it, Lieutenant, an opportunity to explore a primitive world whilst enjoying all mod. cons.! You might never get such a chance again."

"I'll think about it," Grimes told him.

He thought about it. He discussed it with his officers. Mr. Beadle, the First Lieutenant, was not enthusiastic. In spite of his habitual lugubrious mien he had a passion for the bright lights, and made it quite clear that he had enjoyed of late so few opportunities to spend his pay that he could well afford a Gold Coast holiday. Von Tannenbaum, Navigator, Slovotny, Electronic Communications and Vitelli, Engineer sided with Beadle. Grimes did not try to persuade them — after all, he was getting no commission from the Olganan Tourist Bureau. Spooky Deane, the Psionic Communications Officer, asked rather shyly if he could come along with the Captain. He was not the companion that Grimes would have chosen — but he was a telepath, and it was just possible that his gift would be useful.

Deane and Grimes took the rocket mail from Newer York to New Melbourne, and during the trip Grimes indulged in one of his favourite whinges, about the inability of the average colonist to come up with really original names for his cities. At New Melbourne — a drab, oversized village on the southern coast of Never-Never — they stayed at a hotel which, although recommended by Trans-Galactic Clippers, failed dismally to come up to Galactic standards, making no attempt whatsoever to cater for guests born and brought up on worlds with widely differing atmospheres, gravitational fields and dietary customs. Then there was a day's shopping, during which the two spacemen purchased such items of personal equipment as they had been told would be necessary by the office of Never-Never Tours. The following morning, early, they took a cab from their hotel to the Never-Never Coach Terminus. It was still dark, and it was cold, and it was raining.

They sat with the other passengers, all of whom were, like themselves, roughly dressed, in the chilly waiting room, waiting for something to happen. To pass the time Grimes sized up the others. Some were obviously outworlders — there was a TG Clipper in at the spaceport. Some — their accent made it obvious — were Olganans, taking the opportunity of seeing something of their own planet. None of them, on this dismal morning, looked very attractive. Grimes admitted that the same could be said about Deane and himself; the telepath conveyed the impression of a blob of ectoplasm roughly wrapped in a too gaudy poncho.

A heavy engine growled outside, and bright lights stabbed through the big windows. Deane got unsteadily to his feet. "Look at that, Captain!" he exclaimed. "Wheels, yet? I expected an inertial drive vehicle, or at least a hoverbus!"

"You should have read the brochure, spooky. The idea of this tour is to see the country the same way as the first explorers did, to get the *feel* of it . . . "

"I can get the feel of it as well from an aircraft as from

that archaic contraption!"

"We aren't all telepaths . . . "

Two porters had come in and were picking up suitcases, carrying them outside. The tourists, holding their overnight grips, followed, watched their baggage being stowed in a locker at the rear of the coach. From the p.a. system a voice was ordering, "All passengers will now embus! All passengers will now embus!"

The passengers embussed, and Grimes and Deane found themselves seated behind a young couple of obviously Terran origin, while across the aisle from them was a pair of youngish ladies who could be nothing other than schoolteachers. A fat, middle-aged man, dressed in a not very neat uniform of grey coveralls, eased himself into the driver's seat. "All aboard?" he asked. "Anybody who's not, sing out!" The coach lurched from the terminus on to the rain-wet street, was soon bowling north through the dreary suburbs of New Melbourne.

North east they ran at first, and then almost due north, following the coast. Here the land was rich, green, well-wooded, with apple orchards, vineyards, orange groves. Then there was sheep country, rolling downland speckled with the white shapes of the grazing animals. "It's wrong," Deane whispered to Grimes. "It's all wrong . . . "

"What's wrong, Spooky?"

"I can feel it — even if you can't. The . . . the resentment . . . "

"The aborigines, you mean?"

"Yes. But even stronger, the native animals, driven from their own pastures, hunted and destroyed to make room for the outsiders from beyond the stars. And the plants — what's left of the native flora in these parts. Weeds to be rooted out and burned, so that the grapes and grain and the oranges may flourish . . . "

"You must have felt the same on other colonised worlds, Spooky."

"Not as strongly as here. I can almost put it into

139

words . . . *The First Ones* let us alone."

"Mphm," grunted Grimes. "Makes sense, I suppose. The original colonists, with only the resources of *Lode Jumbuk* to draw upon, couldn't have made much of an impression. But when they had all the resources of the Federation to draw upon . . . "

"I don't think it's quite that way . . . " murmured Deane doubtfully.

"Then what *do* you think?"

"I . . . I don't know Captain . . . "

But they had little further opportunity for private talk. Slowly at first, and then more rapidly, the coachload of assorted passengers was thawing out. The driver initiated this process — he was, Grimes realized, almost like the captain of a ship, responsible for the wellbeing, psychological as well as physical, of his personnel. Using a fixed microphone by his seat he delivered commentaries on the places of interest that they passed, and, when he judged that the time was ripe, had another microphone on a wandering lead passed among the passengers, the drill being that each would introduce himself by name, profession and place of residence.

Yes, they were a mixed bag, these tourists. About half of them were from Earth — they must be, thought Grimes, from the TG Clipper *Cutty Sark* presently berthed at the spaceport. Public Servants, lawyers, the inevitable Instructors from universities, both major and minor, improving their knowledge of the worlds of the Federation in a relatively inexpensive way. The Olganans were similarly diversified.

When it came to Grimes' turn he said, "John Grimes, spaceman. Last place of permanent residence St. Helier, Channel Islands, Earth."

Tanya Lancaster, the younger and prettier of the two teachers across the aisle, turned to him. "I thought you were a Terry, John. You don't mind my using your given name, do you? It's supposed to be on the rules on this tour . . . "

"I like it, Tanya."

"That's good. But you can't be from the *Cutty Sark*. I should know all the officers, at least by sight, by this time."

"And if I were one of *Cutty Sark*'s officers," said Grimes gallantly (after all, this Tanya wench was not at all bad looking, with her chestnut hair, green eyes and thin, intelligent face), "I should have known you by this time."

"Oh," she said, "you must be from the Base."

"Almost right."

"You are making things awkward. Ah, I have it. You're from that funny little destroyer or whatever it is that's berthed at the Survey Service's end of the spaceport."

"She's not a funny little destroyer," Grimes told her stiffly. "She's a Serpent Class Courier."

The girl laughed. "And she's *yours*. Yes, I overheard your friend calling you 'Captain' . . . "

"Yes. She's mine . . . "

"And now, folks," boomed the driver's amplified voice, "how about a little singsong to liven things up? Any volunteers?"

The microphone was passed along to a group of young Olganan students. After a brief consultation they burst into song.

"When the jolly *Jumbuk* lifted from Port Woomera
Out and away for Altair Three
Glad were we all to kiss the tired old Earth
goodbye —
Who'll come a-sailing in *Jumbuk* with me?

Sailing in *Jumbuk*, sailing in *Jumbuk*,
Who'll come a-sailing in *Jumbuk* with me?
Glad were we all to kiss the tired old Earth
goodbye —
You'll come a-sailing in *Jumbuk* with me!

Then there was Storm, the Pile and all the engines
dead —
Blown out to Hell and gone were we!
Lost in the Galaxy, falling free in sweet damn all —
Who'll come a-sailing in *Jumbuk* with me?

Sailing in *Jumbuk*, sailing in *Jumbuk*,
Who'll come a-sailing in *Jumbuk* with me?
Lost in the Galaxy, falling free in sweet damn all —
You'll come a sailing in *Jumbuk* with me!

Up jumped the Captain, shouted for his Engineer,
'Start me the diesels, one, two, three!
Give me the power to feed into the Ehrenhafts —
You'll come a-sailing in *Jumbuk* with me!' "

"But that's *ours!*" declared Tanya indignantly, her
Australian accent suddenly very obvious. "It's our
Waltzing Matilda!"

"*Waltzing Matilda* never was yours," Grimes told her.
"The words — yes, but the tune, no. Like many another
song it's always having new verses tacked on to it."

"I suppose you're right. But these comic lyrics of theirs
— what are they all about?"

"You've heard of the Ehrenhaft Drive, haven't you?"

"The first FTL Drive, wasn't it?"

"I suppose you could call it that. The Ehrenhaft
generators converted the ship, the lodejammer, into what
was, in effect, a huge magnetic particle. As long as she
was on the right tramlines, the right line of magnetic force,
she got to where she was supposed to get to in a relatively
short time. But a magnetic storm, tangling the lines of
force like a bowl of spaghetti, would throw her anywhere
— or nowhere. And these storms also drained the
micropile of all energy. In such circumstances all that
could be done was to start up the emergency diesel
generators, to supply electric power to the Ehrenhaft
generators. After this the ship would stooge along

hopefully, trying to find a habitable planet before the fuel ran out . . . ''

"H'm." She grinned suddenly. "I suppose it's more worthy of being immortalised in song than our sheep-stealing Jolly Swagman. But I still prefer the original." And then aided by her friend, Moira Stevens — a fat and cheerful young woman — she sang what she still claimed was the original version. Grimes allowed himself to wonder what the ghost of the Jolly Swagman — still, presumably, haunting that faraway billabong — would have made of it all . . .

That night they reached the first of their camping sites, a clearing in the bush, on the banks of a river that was little more than a trickle, but with quite adequate toilet facilities in plastic huts. The coach crew — there was a cook as well as the driver — laid out the pneumatic pup tents in three neat rows, swiftly inflated them with a hose from the coach's air compressor. Wood was collected for a fire, and folding grills laid across it. "The inevitable steak and billy tea," muttered somebody who had been on the tour before. "It's *always* steak and billy tea . . . "

But the food, although plain, was good, and the yarning around the fire was enjoyable and, finally, Grimes found that the air mattress in his tent was at least as comfortable as his bunk aboard *Adder*. He slept well, and awoke refreshed to the sound of the taped *Reveille.* He was among the first in the queue for the toilet facilities and, dressed and ready for what the day might bring, lined up for his eggs and bacon and mug of tea with a good appetite. Then there was the washing up, the deflation of mattresses and tents, the stowing away of these and the baggage — and, very shortly after the bright sun had appeared over the low hills to the eastward, the tour was on its way again.

On they drove, and on, through drought-stricken land that showed few signs of human occupancy, that was old, old long before the coming of Man. Through sunparched plains they drove, where scrawny cattle foraged listlessly for scraps of sun-dried grass, where tumbleweed scurried

143

across the roadway, where dust-devils raised their whirling columns of sand and light debris. But there was life, apart from the thirsty cattle, apart from the grey scrub that, with the first rains of the wet season, would put forth its brief, vivid greenery, its short-lived gaudy flowers. Once the coach stopped to let a herd of sausagekine across the track — low-slung, furry quadrupeds, wriggling like huge lizards on their almost rudimentary legs. There was a great clicking of cameras. "We're lucky, folks," said the driver. "These beasts are almost extinct. They were classed as pests until only a couple of years ago — now they've been reclassed as protected fauna . . ." They rolled past an aboriginal encampment where gaunt, black figures, looking arachnoid rather than humanoid, stood immobile about their cooking fires. "Bad bastards those," announced the driver. "Most of the others will put on shows for us, will sell us curios — but not that tribe . . . "

Now and again there were other vehicles — diesel-engined tourist coaches like their own, large and small hovercraft and, in the cloudless sky, the occasional high-flying inertial drive aircraft. But, in the main, the land was empty, the long, straight road seeming to stretch to infinity ahead of them and behind them. The little settlements — pub, general store and a huddle of other buildings — were welcome every time that one was reached. There was a great consumption of cold beer at each stop, conversations with the locals, who gathered as though by magic at each halt. There were the coach parks — concentration camps in the desert rather than oases, but with much appreciated hot showers and facilities for washing clothing.

On they drove, and on, and Grimes and Deane teamed up with Tanya and Moira. But there was no sharing of tents. The rather disgruntled Grimes gained the impression that the girl's mother had told her, at an early age, to beware of spacemen. Come to that, after the first two nights there were no tents. Now that they were in regions where it was certain that no rain would fall all hands slept in their sleeping bags only, under the stars.

And then they came to the Cragge Rock reserve. "Cragge Rock," said the driver into his microphone, "is named after Captain Cragge, Master of the *Lode Jumbuk*, just as the planet itself is named after his wife, Olga." He paused. "Perhaps somewhere in the Galaxy there's a mountain that will be called Grimes' Rock — but with all due respect to the distinguished spaceman in our midst he'll have to try hard to find the equal to Cragge Rock! The Rock, folks, is the largest monolith in the known Universe — just a solid hunk of granite. Five miles long, a mile across, half a mile high." He turned his attention to Tanya and Moira. "Bigger than *your* Ayers Rock, ladies!" He paused again for the slight outburst of chuckles. "And to the north, sixty miles distant, there's Mount Conway, a typical mesa. Twenty miles to the south there's Mount Sarah named after Chief Officer Conway's wife. It's usually called 'the Sallies', as it consists of five separate domes of red conglomerate. So you see that geologically Cragge Rock doesn't fit in. There're quite a few theories, folks. One is that there was a submarine volcanic eruption when this was all part of the ocean bed. The Rock was an extrusion of molten matter from the core of the planet. It has been further shaped by millions of years of erosion since the sea floor was lifted to become this island continent."

As he spoke, the Rock was lifting over the otherwise featureless horizon. It squatted there on the skyline, glowering red in the almost level rays of the westering sun, an enormous crimson slug. It possessed beauty of a sort — but the overall impression was one of strength.

"We spend five full days here, folks," went on the driver. "There's a hotel, and there's an abo settlement, and most of the boos speak English. They'll be happy to tell you *their* legends about the Rock — Wuluru they call it. It's one of their sacred places, but they don't mind us coming here as long as we pay for the privilege. That, of course, is all taken care of by the Tourist Bureau, but if you want any curios you'll have to fork out for them . . . See the way that the Rock's changing colour as the sun gets lower? And once the sun's down it'll slowly fade like a dying ember . . . ''

The Rock was close now, towering above them, a red wall against the darkening blue of the cloudless sky. Then they were in its shadow, and the sheer granite wall was purple, shading to cold blue . . . Sunlight again, like a sudden blow, and a last circuit of the time-pocked monolith, and a final stop on the eastern side of the stone mountain.

They got out of the coach, stood there, shivering a little, in the still, chilly air. "It has something . . . " whispered Tanya Lancaster. "it has something . . . " agreed Moira Stevens.

"Ancestral memory?" asked Deane, with unusual sharpness.

"You're prying!" snapped the fat girl.

"I'm not, Moira. But I couldn't help picking up the strong emanation from your minds."

Tanya laughed. "Like most modern Australians we're a mixed lot — and, in our fully integrated society, most of us have some aboriginal blood. But . . . Why should Moira and I feel so at home here, both at home and hopelessly lost?"

"If you let me probe . . . " suggested Deane gently.

"No," flared the girl. "No!"

Grimes sympathized with her. He knew, all too well, what it is like to have a trained telepath, no matter how high his ethical standards, around. But he said, "Spooky's to be trusted. I know."

"You might trust him, John. I don't know him well enough."

"He knows *us* too bloody well!" growled Moira.

"I smell steak," said Grimes, changing the subject.

The four of them walked to the open fire, where the evening meal was already cooking.

Dawn on the Rock was worth waking up early for. Grimes stood with the others, blanket-wrapped against the cold, and watched the great hulk flush gradually from blue to purple, from purple to pink. Over it and beyond it the sky was black, the stars very bright, almost as bright as in airless Space. Then the sun was up, and the Rock stood there, a red island in the sea of tawny sand, a surf of green brush breaking about its base. The show was over. The party went to the showers and toilets and then, dressed, assembled for breakfast.

After the meal they walked from the encampment to the Rock. Tanya and Moira stayed in the company of Grimes and Deane, but their manner towards the two spacemen was distinctly chilly; they were more interested in their guidebooks than in conversation. On their way they passed the aboriginal village. A huddle of crude shelters it was, constructed of natural materials and battered sheets of plastic. Fires were burning, and gobbets of unidentifiable meat were cooking over them. Women — naked, with straggling hair and pendulous breasts, yet human enough — looked up and around at the well-clothed, well-fed tourists with an odd, sly mixture of timidity and boldness. One of them pointed to a levelled camera and screamed, "First gibbit half dollar!"

"You'd better," advised the driver. "Very commercial minded, these people . . . "

Men were emerging from the primitive huts. One of them approached Grimes and his companions, his teeth startlingly white in his coal-black face. He was holding what looked like a crucifix. "Very good," he said, waving it in front of him. "Two dollar."

"I'm not religious . . . " Grimes began, to be cut short by Tanya's laugh.

"Don't be a fool, John," she told him. "It's a throwing weapon."

"A throwing weapon?"

"Yes. Like our boomerangs. Let me show you." She turned to the native, held out her hand. "Here. Please."

"You throw, missie?"

"Yes. I throw."

Watched by the tourists and the natives she held the thing by the end of its long arm, turned until she was facing about forty-five degrees away from the light, morning breeze, the flat surfaces of the cross at right angles to the wind. She raised her arm, then threw, with a peculiar flick of her wrist. The weapon left her hand, spinning, turned so that it was flying horizontally, like a miniature helicopter. It travelled about forty yards, came round in a lazy arc, faltered, then fell in a flurry of fine sand.

"Not very good," complained the girl. "You got better? You got proper one?"

The savage grinned. "You know?"

"Yes. I know."

The man went back into his hut, returned with another weapon. This one was old, beautifully made, and lacking the crude designs that had been burned into the other with redhot wire. He handed it to Tanya, who hefted it approvingly. She threw it as she had thrown the first one — and the difference was immediately obvious. There was no clumsiness in its flight, no hesitation. Spinning, it flew, more like a living thing than a machine. Its arms turned more and more lazily as it came back — and Tanya, with a clapping motion, deftly caught it between her two hands. She stood admiring it — the smooth finish imparted by the most primitive of tools, the polish of age and of long use.

"How much?" she asked.

"No sale, missie." Again the very white grin. "But I give."

"But you can't. You mustn't."

"You take."

"I shouldn't, but . . . "

"Take it, lady," said the driver. "This man is Najatira, the Chief of these people. Refusing his gift would offend him." Then, businesslike, "You guide, Najatira?"

"Yes. I guide." He barked a few words in his own language to his women, one of whom scuttled over the sand to retrieve the first, fallen throwing weapon. Then, walking fast on his big, splayed feet, he strode towards the rock. Somehow the two girls had ranged themselves on either side of him. Grimes looked on disapprovingly. Who was it who had said that these natives were humanoid only? This naked savage, to judge by his external equipment, was all too human. Exchanging disapproving glances, the two spacemen took their places in the little procession.

"Cave," said Najatira, pointing. The orifice, curiously regular, was exactly at the tail of the slug-shaped monolith. "Called, by my people, the Hole of Winds. Story say, in Dream Time, wind come from there, wind move world . . . Before, world no move. No daytime, no night-time . . ."

"Looks almost like a venturi, Captain," Deane remarked to Grimes.

"Mphm. Certainly looks almost too regular to be natural. But erosion does odd things. Or it could have been made by a blast of gases from the thing's inside . . ."

"Precisely," said Deane.

"But you don't think . . . ? No. It would be impossible."

"I don't know what to think," admitted Deane.

Their native guide was leading them around the base of the Rock. "This Cave of Birth. Tonight ceremony. We show you . . . And there — look up. What we call the fishing net. In Dream Time caught big fish . . ."

"A circuit . . ." muttered Grimes. "Exposed by millenia of weathering . . ." He laughed. "I'm getting as bad as you, Spooky. Nature comes up with the most remarkable imitations of Man-made things . . ."

So it went on, the trudge around the base of the monolith, under the hot sun, while their tireless guide pointed out this and that feature. As soon as the older members of the party began to show signs of distress the driver spoke into his wrist transceiver, and within a few minutes the coach came rumbling over the rough track and then, with its partial load, kept pace with those who were still walking. Grimes and Deane were among these hardy ones, but only because Tanya and Moira showed no signs of flagging, and because Grimes felt responsible for the women. After all, the Survey Service had been referred to as the Policemen of the Galaxy. It was unthinkable that two civilized human females should fall for this unwashed savage — but already he knew that civilized human females are apt to do the weirdest things.

At last the tour came to an end. Najatira, after bowing with surprising courtesy, strode off towards his own camp. The tourists clustered hungrily around the folding tables that had been set up, wolfed the thick sandwiches and gulped great draughts of hot, sweet tea.

During the afternoon there were flights over the Rock and the countryside for those who wished them, a large blimp having come in from the nearest airport for that purpose. This archaic transport was the occasion for surprise and incredulity, but it was explained that such aircraft were used by *Lode Jumbuk*'s people for their initial explorations.

"The bloody thing's not safe," complained Deane as soon as they were airborne.

Grimes ignored him. He was looking out and down through the big cabin windows. Yes, the Rock did look odd, out of place. It was part of the landscape — but it did not belong. It had been there for millions of years — but still it did not belong. Mount Conway and Mount Sarah were natural enough geological formations — *but*, he thought, *Cragge Rock was just as natural*. He tried to envision what it must have looked like when that upwelling of molten rock thrust through the ocean bed.

"It wasn't like that, Captain," said Deane quietly.

"Damn you, Spooky! Get out of my mind."

"I'm sorry," the telepath told him, although he didn't sound it. "It's just that this locality is like a jigsaw puzzle. I'm trying to find the pieces, and to make them fit." He looked around to make sure that none of the others in the swaying, creaking cabin was listening. "Tanya and Moira . . . The kinship they feel with Najatira . . ."

"Why don't you ask them about it?" Grimes suggested, jerking his head towards the forward end of the car, where the two girls were sitting. "Is it kinship, or is it just the attraction that a woman on holiday feels for an exotic male?''

"It's more than that.''

"So you're prying.''

"I'm trying not to.'' He looked down without interest at Mount Conway, over which the airship was slowly flying. "But it's hard to.''

"You could get into trouble, Spooky. And you could get the ship into trouble . . . ''

"And you, Captain.''

"Yes. And me.'' Then Grimes allowed a slight smile to flicker over his face. "But I know you. You're on to something. And as we're on holiday from the ship I don't suppose that I can give you any direct orders . . . ''

"I'm not a space-lawyer, so I'll take your word for that.''

"Just be careful. And keep me informed.''

While they talked the pilot of the blimp, his voice amplified, had been giving out statistics. The conversation had been private enough.

That night there was the dance.

Flaring fires had been built on the sand, in a semi-circle, the inner arc of which faced the mouth of the Cave of Birth. The tourists sat there, some on the ground and some on folding stools, the fires at their backs, waiting. Overhead the sky was black and clear, the stars bitterly bright.

From inside the cave there was music — of a sort. There was a rhythmic wheezing of primitive trumpets, the staccato rapping of knocking sticks. There was a yelping male voice — Najatira's — that seemed to be giving orders rather than singing.

Grimes turned to say something to Tanya, but she was no longer in her place. Neither was Moira. The two girls must have gone together to the toilet block; they would be back shortly. He returned his attention to the black entrance to the Cave.

The first figure emerged from it, crouching, a stick held

151

in his hands. Then the second, then the third . . . There was something oddly familiar about it, something that didn't make sense, or that made the wrong kind of sense. Grimes tried to remember what it was. Dimly he realised that Deane was helping him, that the telepath was trying to bring his memories to the conscious level.

Yes, that was it. That was the way that the Marines disembarked on the surface of an unexplored, possibly hostile planet, automatic weapons at the ready . . .

Twelve men were outside the Cave now, advancing in a dance-like step. The crude, tree-stem trumpets were still sounding, like the plaint of tired machinery, and the noise of the knocking sticks was that of cooling metal. The leader paused, stood upright. With his fingers in his mouth he gave a piercing whistle.

The women emerged, carrying bundles, hesitantly, two steps forward, one step back. Grimes gasped his disbelief. Surely that was Tanya, as naked as the others — and there was no mistaking Moira. He jumped to his feet, ignoring the protests of those behind him, trying to shake off Deane's restraining hand.

"Let go!" he snarled.

"Don't interfere, Captain!" The telepath's voice was urgent. "Don't you see? They've gone native — no, that's not right. But they've reverted. And there's no law against it."

"I can still drag them out of this. They'll thank me after." He turned around and shouted, "Come on, all of you! We must put a stop to this vile performance!"

"Captain Grimes!" This was the coach driver, his voice angry. "Sit down, sir! This sort of thing has happened before, and it's nothing to worry about. The young ladies are in no danger!"

"It's happened before," agreed Deane, unexpectedly. "With neurotic exhibitionists, wanting to have their photographs taken among the savages. But not *this* way!"

Then, even more unexpectedly, it was Deane who was running out across the sand, and it was Najatira who advanced to meet him, not in hostility but in welcome. It was Grimes who, unheeded, yelled, "Come back, Spooky! Come back here!"

He didn't know what was happening, but he didn't like it. First of all those two silly bitches, and now one of his own officers. What the hell was getting into everybody? Followed by a half dozen of the other men he ran towards the cave mouth. Their way was barred by a line of the tribesmen, holding their sticks now like spears (which they were) — not like makebelieve guns. Najatira stood proudly behind the armed men, and on either side of him stood the two girls, a strange, arrogant pride in every line of their naked bodies. And there was Deane, a strange smile on his face. His face, too, was strange, seemed suddenly to have acquired lines of authority.

"Go back, John," he ordered. "There is nothing that you can do." He added softly, "But there is much that I can do."

"What the hell are you talking about, Spooky?"

"I'm an Australian, like Moira and Tanya here. Like them, I have the Old Blood in my veins. Unlike them, I'm a spaceman. Do you think that after all these years in the Service I, with my talent, haven't learned how to handle and navigate a ship, any ship? I shall take my people back to where they belong."

And then Grimes *knew*. The knowledge came flooding into his mind, from the mind of Deane, from the minds of the others, whose ancestral memories had been awakened by the telepath. But he was still responsible. He must still try to stop this craziness.

"Mr Deane!" he snapped as he strode forward firmly. He brushed aside the point of the spear that was aimed at his chest. He saw Tanya throw something, and sneered as it missed his head by inches. He did not see the cruciform boomerang returning, was aware of it only as a crashing blow from behind, as a flash of crimson light, then darkness.

He recovered slowly. He was stretched out on the sand beside the coach. Two of the nurses among the passengers were with him.

153

He asked, as he tried to sit up, "What happened?"

"They all went back into the cave," the girl said. "The rock . . . The rock closed behind them. And there were lights. And a voice, it was Mr. Deane's voice, but loud, loud, saying, 'Clear the field? Clear the field! Get back, everybody. Get well back. Get well away!' So we got well back."

"And what's happening now?" asked Grimes. The nurses helped him as he got groggily to his feet. He stared towards the distant Rock. He could hear the beat of mighty engines and the ground was trembling under his feet. Lights flashed here and there on the surface of the monolith. Even with the knowledge that Deane had fed into his mind he could not believe what he was seeing.

The Rock was lifting, its highest part suddenly eclipsing a bright constellation. It was lifting, and the skin of the planet protested as the vast ship, that for so long had been embedded in it, tore itself free. Tremors knocked the tourists from their feet, but somehow Grimes remained standing, oblivious to the shouts and screams. He heard the crash behind him as the coach was overturned, but did not look. At this moment it was only a minor distraction.

The Rock was lifting, had lifted. It was a deeper blackness against the blackness of the sky, a scattering of strange, impossible stars against the distant stars, a bright cluster (at first) that dimmed and diminished, that dwindled, faster and faster, and then was gone, leaving in its wake utter darkness and silence.

The silence was broken by the coach driver. He said slowly, "I've had to cope with vandalism in my time, but nothing like this. What the Board will say when they hear that their biggest tourist attraction has gone I hate to think about . . . " He seemed to cheer up slightly. "But it was one of *your* officers, Captain Grimes, from *your* ship, that did it. I hope you enjoy explaining it!"

Grimes explained, as well as he was able, to Commander Lewin.

He said, "As we all know, sir, there are these odd races, human rather than humanoid, all through the

Galaxy. It all ties in with the Common Origin of Mankind theories. I never used to have much time for them myself, but now . . . "

"Never mind that, Grimes. Get on with the washing."

"Well, Deane was decent enough to let loose a flood of knowledge into my mind just before that blasted Tanya clonked me with her boomerang. It seems that millions of years ago these stone spaceships, these hollowed out asteroids, were sent to explore this Galaxy. I got only a hazy idea of their propulsive machinery, but it was something on the lines of our Inertial Drive, and something on the lines of our Mannschenn Drive, with auxiliary rockets for manoeuvring in orbit and so forth. They were never meant to land, but they could, if they had to. Their power? Derived from the conversion of matter, any matter, with the generators or converters ready to start up when the right button was pushed — but the button had to be pushed psionically. Get me?"

"Not very well. But go on."

"Something happened to this ship, to the crew and passengers of this ship. A disease, I think it was, wiping out almost all the adults, leaving only children and a handful of not very experienced ratings. Somebody — it must have been one of the officers just before he died — got the ship down somehow. He set things so that it could not be re-entered until somebody with the right qualifications came along."

"The right qualifications?"

"Yes. Psionic talents, more than a smattering of astronautics, and descended from the Old People . . . "

"Like your Mr. Deane. But what about the two girls?"

"They had the Old Blood. And they were highly educated. And they could have been latent telepaths . . . "

"Could be." Levin smiled without much mirth. "Meanwhile, Lieutenant, I have to try to explain to the Olganan Government, with copies to Trans-Galactic Clippers *and* to our own masters, including *your* Commodore Damien. All in all, Grimes, it was a fine night's work. Apart from the Rock, there were two TG

155

passengers *and* a Survey Service officer . . . ''

''*And* the tribe . . . ''

''The least of the Olganan Government's worries, and nothing at all to do with TG or ourselves. Even so . . . '' This time his smile was tinged with genuine, but sardonic, humour.

''Even so?'' echoed Grimes.

''What if those tribesmen and women decided to liberate — I suppose that's the right word — those other tribespeople, the full-blooded ones who're still living in the vicinity of the other stone spaceship? What if the Australians realise, one sunny morning, that their precious Ayers Rock has up and left them?''

''I know who'll be blamed,'' said Grimes glumly.

''How right you are,'' concurred Lewin.

GROWING UP

Damien Broderick

I

Afloat in her aninertial field, the child dreams. A breath of subtle particles wafts through her flesh and bone, responsive to every pulse and matrix of her central nervous system. Guardian machines sensitive as flowers to the sun's warmth inhale that fragrance, tropic to the contours and gradients of her sleeping thoughts. They sense the flux and burgeoning of her adolescence, the chemistry of her pubescent mind. She dreams of dancing.

The gracious moving figures are vivid, defined, precise; the *taiko* gongs, and the wind instruments play at *Oibuki*, pursuing independently their same melody, toning in complexity to the next beat, the next unison, and departing once more into contained autonomy; Sriyanie sees and hears this clearly, comes with the other dancers from the greenroom as the *Gagaku* orchestra brings *jo* to conclusion; yet she is distinct from them also, at once immanent and detached, spectator and creator, her dreaming self the stage.

Her dream approaches lucidity. Almost, her state of consciousness is bifurcate. This condition, indeed, is an elementary discipline of the Third Level, and the child, the young woman, is on the verge of passage to Fourth Level; but Sriyanie has not intended lucidity, and the watchful machines detect her disquiet.

Under a pale green sky, many children watch the *Bugaku* dance in awed delight. They whisper to one another; several hold hands, the youngest stir with a certain restlessness. Upon the great platform is a damask-carpeted stage, and the black and red of the platform's perimeter gleam against the grass of the meadow. The dancers move to a largo pace, then quicken their steps as the second movement, *ha*, is begun. Sriyanie watches joyfully; in her dream, Sriyanie dances: the gorgeous Heian costumes, red, purple and gold, the bright flowers in her hair, the flashing shifts of hue as the dancers disclose the hidden inner sleeves of their gowns.

Sriyanie is a bird, adrift. She knows ("she" "knows") that this is *Warawa-mai*, the children's *bugaku*, a Left-dance, elegant and slow; her departure, in truth, from Third Level. She dances to a melody older than machines, older at any rate than any machine she has ever known, and its *Ichikotsucho* mode is alien to the musical canon of her people, for it is based in a tetrachord; yet she has lived now with *Karyobin*, the bird, for many months, and the archaic Nipponese music is an intimate caress across five thousand years, binding her with its patterned beauty.

That contiguity, somehow, is alarming. The orchestration of her sleeping brain peaks and trembles; sadness and loss suffuse the images of grace. Elsewhere, awake, the child's Friend is informed of her grief, and lifts herself sighing to her feet, strangely moved by her little girl's readiness to leave childhood behind. Beth speaks without words to the guardian machines, and goes out into the chill night air. Third Level youngsters are not permitted Transit; for Friends, walking is an obligatory act of praise.

The *kakko* player strikes his side-drum. They are in the *kyu* movement, dancing allegretto, the *sho* sounding to its player's breath, the tiny *hichiriki* piping like a soul in agony, like the *Kalavinka*, the magic bird; in its complex entirety, the music drones, it drones exquisitely. The dance is near its end. Gong and drum announce their coda of percussion. The splendid, gentle dance is done; Sriyanie is exhausted and elated, transfigured; the child is asleep and the dance is in the child, is done, is in the past, is the past; Sriyanie's eyes still their blind dance, and she stirs, groaning, waking, the aninertial field holding her weightless and aloft as she wakes, her mood confused and resentful. Beth is waiting in the dim light, and takes her to her breast.

She holds the child at arm's length, then, and regards her with loving patience. Sriyanie smiles ruefully, knuckling sleep from her eyes, drops her hand to her lap and gazes at them. "I felt so sad, Ummy. Did I wake you?" Through the foul, scudding haze overhead, a handful of stars glint.

"I was making colours, sweet," Beth says, touching a loose lock of the girl's white hair. "You know I don't mind. Would you like to tell me, or should I withdraw for a little while?"

Sriyanie smiles again, a sudden radiance. She puts her arms about her Other and hugs her tightly. "I love you, Beth. Please stay."

For a time they sit in silence, the older woman sinking into a receptive meditation, attending to the background thutter of the machines as they cherish the child's integrity, watching her face through half-closed eyes, adding colours to her own private composition. "I saw the reality of *mujokan*," the girl says at last, slowly. "The, the fleeting impermanence of our lives, of our work. I dreamed the bird dance, and I saw how beautiful it was, and I thought of those silly, lovely Heian people drifting to extinction like falling cherry blossoms, all governed by tact and taste and ritual, and how their freedom was, was isomorphic to the rules of their world, and, I guess, how the Lords contain us under the bounds of possibility, knowing so infinitely much more than we can, weaving their vast dark patterns out between the stars, and we're watching from beyond the platform, hardly understanding any of it, and what's worse even the *Lords* are bound by limitations of their own, oh, grand limits we can't even begin to imagine, but bounded in their cold freedom, and Beth, it was so sad.''

Her Friend looks at her with grave, tender concern. She says at last: ''There's a scene in one of Chikamatsu's plays, *Love Suicides at Soneyaki*, where the lovers begin their final journey. Do you know it, Sri?''

Blinking her tearful eyes, the child shakes her head.

''It goes like this,'' her Other says, in Old Nipponese:

'' 'Farewell to this world
and to the night, farewell.
We who walk the way to death,
to what should we be likened?
To the frost on the road
to the graveyard
vanishing with each
step ahead:
This dream of a dream
is sorrowful.' ''

The Friend falls silent, tranquil, the words whispering away into the night. Sriyanie rocks back and forth, crosslegged, taking the ancient lamentation into herself. Then, once more, she begins to grin, and sees that Beth is grinning, and her hand steals into her Other's.

''You sly person, Ummy. Will you play Zen Master tonight? Well, I suppose an atrocious pun is better than a blow across the head.'' She adopts a reverent expression and intones the final lines as though they followed the phonemic rules of Mid-English, her special area:

'' '*Yume no yume koso
aware nare.*'
'This dream of a dream
is aware.' ''

She pulls a face, and jumps to her feet. Beth rises too, and gives a small bow. ''I thought you'd like it. But it is a useful joke. Awareness replaces sorrow, Sri. I don't mean we should disguise and bind our emotions under a carapace of thought. But on a metalevel we know a reality larger than small losses and achievements. We must grieve for a death, but it is foolish to grieve for a life.''

Barefoot, they walk in wet grass, sleeping flowers crinkling beneath their toes. A luminous theorem glows like fire in the sky about the Fifth's arena, its axioms flickering in a gorgeous aurora of transformations. Sriyanie's melancholy is dispelled in the crisp night; her breath puffs on the air; she feels a rush of love for her Friend, her friends, her world. Even the brooding ubiquity of the cyborg Lords, their energies cracking through the world like an invisible, inaudible electric storm, does not blight this new acceptance. They come to Beth's privacy, and the domestic machines welcome them with warm odours and warming vibrations. Beth leads her through a dull red shield to the Transit locus, then faces her for a moment, holding both her hands.

"Let's go see the sunrise on the beach at Suva," Sri's Other suggests buoyantly, and the tiny cues of her body, the minute pressures of her fingers, are saying suddenly in an urgent kinesic tongue: *Trust me, open yourself, expect change; little love, trust me.*

"Transit! Am I ready? How wonderful," the girl says dubiously. "I'm hungry, Beth, are you? Shall we have fish?"

Beth nods, and the scintillation of Transit discontinuity sings in their bodies; Sriyanie steps forward, expecting beyond the filtration field the boom of waves, the greasy, mother-of-pearl gloss of the ocean, the bustle of people in the new day, a tang of fish on coals —

— Nullity. Blank void, nothingness, unspeakable gulf of numb, black, weightless nowhere —

The child screams in terror, and there is no sound. Her mind is trapped in dread, flailing without motion, draining to some nadir of horror which is total inaction. In the instantaneous no-time before awareness is finally lost, she clings to the memory of her Other's hand: *Trust me, little one, trust me.*

Anomic, her central field of consciousness, of being, sustains appalling paradox. Tenuous as vapour, a quintessence, she is dissipated in infinite void. Simultaneously she undergoes catastrophic implosion, the

161

multistable universe recedes to oblivion, she suffers ultimate, singular density. Suspended, dispersed, a frail bubble of grotesque mass, her being drones to some complex derivative of the august cosmic inertial frame.

It is dark, dark, deepest red. What are these forms, limpid, fugative, a geometry of edges limned in gold and purple, gentle pressures, passing from nowhere to nowhere? She rocks back and forth, slowly, slowly, to booming, delayed echoes. Bright stars reel past sunbursts tasting of gems. Light ebbs in sluggish waves, rolling in pale bands and bands of darkness. Percussions rise and fall, climbing, pounding through bone and nerve as glimmer makes vast shadows grow and thrum and dominate her rhythms like the throb of an ocean, like a primordial heartbeat . . .

Reality is a cage, a comforting restraint of vertical shafts, an irksome debility. She is depleted, miserable; she draws the warmth and the soft pale glow to herself, encloses it within her. Brightness regards her. Gratitude surges within her like a tide. There is Another. She reaches for the warmth, crooning with love, holding to that trust she had almost failed, and recognizes Beth.

Ummy, she says, *Ummy, hold me.*

Sri, her Other says, *I love you, I love you.*

Painfully, exuberantly, she rebuilds her world. The void is not without form; at one pole she retains herself, at the other her Other; between them, the pulse of energy elaborates its grid, its field, its intricate, manifold relationships, its matrix. Does she build the world? Does the world disclose itself to her? She sees that both are true. She takes colours from the void and shapes them; they tint the patterns of the void. Many people laugh. Many people speak, disputing. Many people weep. She has invented them all. Beth is with her. She is not Beth. She is like Beth. She is like herself. She likes herself, and Beth, and the universe they have built. She turns, withdraws, broods, grows unhappy with her work. Why must Beth plague her with her presence? Violently, she repulses her Other. She modifies her work, tampers with its shape. She feels pain. She feels joy. She cannot find

Beth, and she weeps, tasting salt. She is in the sea, and the salt fills her mouth, her hard teeth snapping against a melancholy of blood.

Ummy, she cries, *hold my hand.*

The world jigs and capers. In the gibbering confusion, Beth grips her hand. Strata slide and grind, horrendously. She constructs taxa, and pays the toll. She giggles and groans. Expectation swells within her, seethes; she tenses her muscles and fixes her gaze, and holds Beth's hand in her own, and leaps —

They tumble together into sand. Sriyanie hoots, turns her shoulder into the hot white sand (hot?) and goes heels-over-head, comes up snorting and flops to her knees to stare at the crashing white waves in the endless, surging ocean. Beth brushes sand from her own hair and examines small dry shells. Sriyanie runs heavily to the edge of the water and dips her toes into clear, frothy ripples (clear?).

"Wow," she says, scanning out to sea. Tiny white sails dance at the deep horizon. "It's *beautiful*. Where's the pollution gone?" Her face creases; she says in puzzlement, turning, "Hey, Ummy, there was something weird about —"

Dread, like nightmare, assails her. The sun has been up for hours. Beth sits cross-legged on the sand beside a glowing fire-pit. Silvery fat fish wrapped in large leaves char on the coals. Sampling a glass of some sparkling liquid, Beth holds the bottle out towards her.

"Breakfast'll be ready in a moment, Sri," Beth tells her. "Come and sit by me. We're not in Suva, pet."

"Where did the *fire* come from?" she says shrilly. "Is this a cyborg simulation?" She stares at the pit in horror, knowing that it is not a simulation, knowing that Beth would not have brought her to a simulation. Her loathing is ghastly in its effect: the fire is no longer there, it has never been there. Beth rises from the unmarked white sand and comes to her as she stands trembling.

"Too fast, pet? But now we have no breakfast. Look," she gestures, and the fish are there again, cooked now and piled on a woven platter. "I made it up, Sri. Then you unmade it. But it's real, Sri. Hang onto that. Here, have something to eat." She picks up a fish, gingerly, and takes a bit, then hands it to the girl. "Mmm." Beth licks her lips. "Tasty. Try some, you'll like it."

Sriyanie takes the fish and places it between her teeth. The aroma is superb. She bites, and the white flesh is firm. She cannot bring herself to swallow it, and spits her mouthful on to the sand. She remembers how she and Beth built the world, and the knowledge is too awesome, too large to absorb.

"We made it up?" she says in a small voice. "We made all this up?"

"Well, sort of," Beth says, smiling at last. "You did most of it. I just helped tidy up the edges."

"Where are we Beth? Beth, am I still asleep?"

"We call it Timestop, pet. Our duration is orthogonal to the prime metrodynamic. We've shunted out of Transit, and we can stay here as long as we like before we go back. It's basically Third Level Math, but you won't really appreciate all of it until Fifth. Sriyanie," she adds, proud and formal, "you've now been initiated into the first of the Great Mysteries. We'll be moving across to Fourth as soon as we get back from Suva." The formality vanishes, and she hugs the girl tightly. "Now, eat your fish, and we'll see what we can dream up to drink with it."

Sriyanie squats in the sand and retracts her attention. Her heart is pounding; absently, she slows her tachycardia, hushes the thousand anxious voices of her autonomic system. An immense joy sweeps her. Her profoundly trained mind — now that Beth's calculated, shocking challenge has been met — sorts and matches what she has learned with what she has known. The epistemological requirements for this apparently insane ontology map themselves outward and inward from her painstakingly provisional verities. She sees how Timestop is possible. She discerns gaps where she has never noticed them before; they are immediately self-evident; immediately, also, the bridging transformations generate themselves. Her joy is a tranquil exultation. She sees how Timestop is inevitable.

"The Lords do not know," she posits quietly:

In mathematical notation: "Cyborg percept-concept-action structures," Beth tells her, "are categorically prohibited from this condition."

"Then we are truly free," the child breathes. "They have limits we do not. Beth, Beth, why didn't you *tell* me?"

"You were not ready," her Other says; she speaks, of course, in chomsky, the basic language she shares with Sriyanie and the other Frees: the loops and structures of her utterance provide their own unassailable conviction. "Besides," she adds, "there are societal restraints, as well as epistemological ones. The cyborgs must never learn about Timestop. It is our only retreat, our minimal advantage. One day, hopefully, we shall learn enough to make it more than that. But for now, the ontological access of Transit discontinuity must remain a secret. Do you see?"

"Yes, Beth," says the girl, and withdraws once more, her thoughts accelerating, the webs of concept and action broadening and growing robust. Above her, the sun moves toward noon in the improbably clear sky. Sweat springs from her skin, trickles in her armpits. The wine is clean and tart on her tongue; she puts down her glass and shades her eyes, glorying in the universe she has hewn with Beth.

"Let me tell you a story," her Other says, turning over and digging her elbows into the sand. "It's a very old tale, one of the oldest we know. Have you heard of Oedipus, the Swollen-Footed King?"

"I don't think so. A Greek lord?"

"One of the mythic figures of the archaic Hellenic culture," Beth says. "His father was Laios, the Left-sided; his grandfather, Labdakos, the Lame. These ascriptions, as you can see, were metonymic. Well, the story goes this way. Laios is banished from Thebes and develops a homosexual relationship with the charioteer Chrysippos, his patron's son. In time he returns to his throne, marries Jokaste, but refrains from heterosex because an oracle reveals that her son will kill him. During a fertility rite, though, Laios grows drunk and lustful, and

165

Oedipus is conceived.

"The baby is consigned, with orders for his murder, to a herdsman, but the executioner relents and merely stakes the child by his foot to a chilly mountaintop. Before Oedipus can perish from exposure, a peasant finds him and rears him in secrecy. Years later, the adult Oedipus returns to Thebes in a chariot, and encounters Laios on his way to the Delphic oracle. In an argument over right of precedence on the road, Laios causes Oedipus's horse to be slain; in fury, and ignorant of their relationship, his son kills him. The prophecy has been borne out.

"Subsequently, the road to Thebes is terrorized by the Sphinx, a monster with the body of a beast and the torso of a woman. To win the widowed Queen's hand, Oedipus meets the monster in contest. He is riddled: 'What creature goes in the morning on four feet, at noon on two, and in the evening on three?' He answers correctly: 'Man.' In mortification, the Sphinx suicides.

"For many years Oedipus reigns in Thebes, fathering children by Jokaste, his all-unknown mother. As you can see, the chronology is somewhat strained; the ancient Greeks had no anti-agathics. At last Thebes is afflicted with plague and famine. An oracle reveals the cause: the royal incest, and the parricide which preceded it. Jokaste takes her own life and Oedipus goes mad, tearing out his eyes. He leaves the city once again, attended only by his daughter Antigone, and himself attains supernatural insight."

Beth falls silent. Sriyanic has been listening with keen interest, playing sand through her fingers. Now she gazes at the dazzling waves, and muses.

"It's lovely, Beth," she says at last. "Austere and terribly sombre. I think I'll suggest it for a Being-Them." She sucks at her lip. "I suppose Antigone came back to Thebes and took the throne?"

"No. Oedipus had sons also, it was very rare for women to rule."

"Oh. Then I imagine the rightful heir was driven out, and came back eventually to seize the crown?"

"Something like that. If I remember properly, Eteokles banished Polyneikes, who brought back an army, and both the contending brothers were killed. You see something cyclical, then?"

"Beth, it's so rich in resonances I don't know which harmonic to start with. It taps right into the deep structures. But look: if it's a myth, it can't stand by itself. It's just one element in a huge redundant mosaic, and anything I say must be so partial —"

"Naturally. But Sri, myth is also holonic. Within the larger context, each part has its own integrity. Tell me what you got."

"Well, right, the basic structure's cyclical, but it's also paradoxical. And there are strong cybernetic elements: the road to Thebes is obviously part of a prime information circuit, a model for data-and-decisions, and the Sphinx catapults that up to a metalevel. I mean, hodological routes are the most blatant symbols any low-mobility culture can use to work out their problems with internal and external dynamics. Then there's that beautiful econic loop, where the urban child is taken to doom by the pastoral intermediary and saved by the agrarian benefactor, and comes back to master the town, and ends up transfigured again in the rural domain."

Beth considers her through a mesh of lashes. "Low-mobility cultures also placed great store by kinship regulations."

"Oh, sure," the girl says dismissively. "There's that whole strident incest thing, with Laios symbolically fucking his son, and Oedipus actually fucking his mother, and their town getting the pox. That's a surface reading, Beth, though I dare say the retailers did plenty of winking and nudging. What fascinates me is the deep resonance. You know, it's incredible: the whole thing's about us and the cyborgs. The dreadful road to high technology, where it leads and the way out. Maybe the way out."

"You understood the meaning of the Sphinx's riddle?"

Sriyanie preens. "I know about walking-sticks. And chariots. Yes, Beth. Man begins as an animal, passes

167

through a bipedal state of simple culture, freeing his hands to use tools, and finally leans so heavily on his technology that it's completely introjected. Actually," she says with surprise, "I guess that's true of individuals, too: crawling on all fours as babies . . ."

She trails off, and immense shock shows in her face. Abruptly, she jumps to her feet and runs to the sea, discarding her robe, and splashes wildly in the ebbing tide. Waistdeep, she submerges, comes up coughing, light glinting from her pale body. The water lifts her like an aninertial field, tugs her gently toward the long dark line of the horizon. Shrieking in delight she turns, paddling clumsily, forges to the shore, races in a dog-legged curve of deep footprints back to Beth.

"It's all about me," she gasps, out of breath, flat on her back. "Me and Timestop and that weird thing that happened. Ummy, you *are* sly! It's a myth of the individual's saccadic development."

"Bravo!" Beth applauds. "Don't give me too much credit for ingenuity, though. The old psychologists recognized as much thousands of years ago. They even used it to denominate the principal inputs of individuation: the Oedipus Nexus."

"Yes! Yes!" Sriyanie cried. "So lots of the details are apotropaic, to incorporate the metalevels. Old Swollen-Foot begins in the sensori-motor stage — and one limb is crippled! He develops through magic omnipotence, climaxing his journey through the pre-operational stage by killing his father. To attain the powers of adulthood, he must deal at the concrete operational level with a riddle — and the riddle, of course, is a rebus for the entire myth, combining individual and cultural development. Then, when he finally passes into the formal operational stage of adulthood, his insight into the abstract kinship transgression of his marriage hurls him into mystical consciousness. It's all elided, but it's all there."

She is fairly bouncing with delight. "He tears out his eyes, because they are the organs of guilty perception — which takes us right back to his crime, since the baby's earliest social transaction was with his mother, through their mutual gaze. And mystical insight requires a new metalevel anyway, passing beyond rigorous formal operations into antinomies. It's devastating, Beth! How sublimely those old savages captured it all!''

Her drying hair clings to her scalp like pale fronds. Beth musses it, and gets to her feet. All trace of their repast is gone. "They weren't really savages, Sri. They were at the very edge of the path leading to the cities, to the thinking machines. I imagine, though, they had no inkling of Timestop. That had to wait until metrodynamic discontinuity. Why do you think the story is about you?''

They climb the sandhills, away from the beach. Insects buzz among the flowering grasses, the tropical trees.

"Well, this potential matrix we're in was built up the same way. I knew you were with me, but I felt omnipotent — and lost. Then the phylogenetic codes came snapping in, one by one, and everything sort of . . . crystallized.'' She stops, perched on one leg, and looks searchingly at her Other. "What would've happened if I'd come through here on my own? I'd have used psychosis, wouldn't I?''

"If you'd got here," Beth agrees. "I doubt that you would have been able to; it's a complicated trick, and only a very stable, imaginative adult mind can originate it. Youngsters entering Fourth Level are guided in, as I did with you. But if a child *did* come through without support — well, it's a horrifying thought. Total solipsism, I suppose. The reality we generate here is stabilized by consensus, and that includes all our sophisticated social constraints as well as the phylogenetic deep structures.''

The child shivers. She plucks a ripe fruit from a tree, and bites into it. Rich, luscious juice covers her chin.

"You said this was the first of the Great Mysteries," she says thoughtfully. "Ummy, when am I to be initiated into the rest? Or shouldn't I ask?''

Her Other reaches up, takes a fruit from the same tree. "The Second Mystery is greater than the First," she says. She eats the fruit slowly, regarding Sriyanie. Like a mother, then, like a priest, she lays her hands upon the girl's shoulders.

The world fades back into forms without content, into lines and points of vivid hue. They are suspended in the void once more. Beth's gaze is warm and bright, tranquil. The bond between them streams with light. Beth's soul opens: her childhood, her growing-up in the embrace of her own Friend, her abundant adulthood, her being. Trembling, the child enters the door.

Sriyanie is Beth, is Beth, is Beth.

II

Inevitably (and thus, the Lords being as they are, in its specifics diabolically adventitious) the summons comes for Sriyanie when she is most vulnerable, disarmed by a yielding passion. Drowsing, she's boneless and spent in the tangled tumble of her Five. Yuri turns slightly, nuzzled into the crook of Kolpias' heavy arm; his shin presses Sriyanie's gratingly, breaking her imaged reverie, and she too shifts a little, bringing her face around into the hairy curve of Guillaume's belly. The greater curve of the Blue Torus blurs in counterpoint. Guillaume's shrunken penis lolls in sticky fur; Sriyanie takes it in her hand and lifts her voice in a teasing, sweet soprano:

"Ah, sweet mystery of life —" and holds the note until her voice shivers in tremolo.

Brolga prises herself up from the knot, frowns, returns to meditation. Kolpias guffaws, his brutal chest shaking, and Yuri starts from sleep, snorts, sniggers as the note dies, grabs at Sriyanie's nose to blatt the rest. Guillaume gazes slyly down at them, retrieves his prick from Sriyanie's clasp and cups it piously, completes the line in creditable falsetto:

"— At last I've found thee!"

They all break up, even Brolga, and fall with one accord on Guillaume, pummelling his naked flesh, grasping in threat and mock lust at the eponymous mystery. He wriggles free, springs to his feet, scampers with much display of terror to the sonic zone of the Torus and repels their attack with a lurid, deafening arpeggio. But Kolpias has him by the ankles and pulls him down; Sriyanie has found a kilo of fat crinkled peanuts, and rains them on his hapless head; Brolga interposes herself in his defense, kneels, takes the mystery between her lips, reverently, and the mood is altered in a trice: Sriyanie is elevated in a daze of helpless love for these four. They cease their capers. Gently, they caress one another's flesh. The Torus is alert; its blue light softens, and the tug of gravity fades: they float, enraptured and in love, and the cyborg Darkstar enters their joy without warning, terrible and ineluctable, to bear Sriyanie away.

Here is the event's most dreadful aspect: she has known it will come, has expected it daily and hourly, and has denied it. Even in this moment of its actuality she backs off, trembling, bringing up her palms; some weak link of her will traduces her, saps courage from her perception of *what is*; the cyborg Lord comes to her from the Torus Transit locus, and she shrinks away.

He pads forward proudly, imperious, claws glinting as they show and retract between white tufts of downy fur. He has the guise of a huge chinchilla cat, his eyes pale chrysoprase slit by vertical dark emptiness, stiff grey hair along the spine, tail thick and white, aloft, white as the dense, beautiful fur of his body. His voice wheezes and rasps: "Come, pretty one; come, child," and his tongue is rose-pink and minutely scaled.

Sriyanie puts her hands by her sides, and breathes. The Four of her Five are frozen in postures of hatred and resignation. She is the first of them to be called. Her waiting has not been extensive, after all, yet she cannot believe it is at an end. Beth has prepared her; she finds herself unready. Her new love denies it, denies it.

The cat lifts on its back legs, half her height, and lays its paws against her. She does not recoil. "Sriyanie N'Zanvy, you are called. Are you ready for your season in heaven?"

Kolpias will hold back no longer. With an animal cry, he lunges at the biofacted cat. The Lord whirls, rakes his cheek. The man staggers and falls, tiny globes of blood leaping in five lines on his pale flesh. The Darkstar turns once more. "Woman, you will come. Let us leave this place with dignity."

She is not permitted to go to Kolpias. He sprawls unconscious in blue light, blood standing purple on his cheek. She would kiss them all, would weep; it is not allowed. She has been expecting this moment ever since the anti-agathics technicians released her from the extended latency plateau. She is an adult; it is not forever, after all. With their eyes the others make her promises she knows they cannot keep. We shall wait for you; our hearts shall remember, and lay themselves open to your absence, and yearn for your return. They believe what their eyes tell her, but she knows that it does not work that way. Her first love is lost, is stolen, is spoiled in an attrition not yet begun but inevitable. Her breast aches as she follows the cat to the locus; she chokes with grief. The shrilling of Transit makes her anew in another place, and the Four are gone; she is here and they are there, sobbing and raging tending Kolpias' perfunctory wound. Misery closes her throat and her vision.

After a time she says: "You are inhuman. You are inhuman."

Four Nest adults stand at a respectful distance. In their faces is excitement and expectation. The cat lifts its great green-golden eyes to her, and says: "We are transhuman, child. We are entelechies. Come, now, and greet your new companions. Your life has begun."

Finally (to be blunt) we are straining empathy to the shearing point. Sriyanie's *Dasein*, her being-in-the world, is outrageous enough, but that of the Darkstar's retinue is grotesque, unconscionable, even by her distended standards.

Let's leave it at this: *I'm* staring through a tiny crack in the wall, and *you're* straining to get some sense out of my muttered reports; we make use of what we can get, which is better than nothing.

So consider Sriyanie in the Darkstar's den, attended by the blithe sprites of the Lord's retinue, or six handsful of them, at a time, in rotation. She's sullen and moody for a period, disdainful, unco-operative (and who can blame her?), but again we're in trouble. Neither Sriyanie nor the hivers count time as we do. We lack even a meaningful common chronology.

On the Outside, under the filtration fields, the Free people keep at least the rudiments of solar, lunar, sidereal cycles. But the world is long since razed to a monocrop of weeds amid filth, choked by millennia of high-energy waste, a catastrophic ecology of entropy. If their bodies still tick to the fluctuations and triggering jabs of that off-centre precession, sun-and-closest-planets (an astrology long since assimilated in their biophysics), it is held of less account than the more intimate seasons of individual attainment: those quantal leaps of concept rehearsed by initiates in the fecund void of Timestop. Their yardstick is the Levels, a calendar relativistic as any starship's clock. In a sense they have returned to Sacred, as distinct from Profane, time; more accurately, it is Human rather than Industrial.

Bizarre? Unwieldy? Not by comparison. For the cyborgs' little doves and hinds time zings like an elastic band. Hook your head into teratotechnology, and the data-bits fly with winged feet; galaxies zoom in your skull like randy bugs; or, if you prefer, primary partons grind to a halt, fuzzy in a dew of probability amplitudes, so that you may scale their crags and bounce in their pools. Time is, to all intents and purposes, obliterated. History is generating inside those awesome CPUs so many googol-times faster than fleshy cells can conceive that its human specification is without meaning.

Sriyanie's term as hostage/tourist/pupil in the cyborg domain comes (as for all Frees, borrowed briefly and replaced) at a critical period. On a rising curve into maturity, her trajectory has been interrupted. Everything shrieks at this violence, yet there is nothing palpable to repudiate. Anger fades; finally she is prepared to debate, at least, with her cloyingly sweet sentries.

"Your lives are a travesty," she tells Livani dully. He props his stained-glass chin on his knuckles and considers her tolerantly. "You are an abrogation of everything decent in myth and history."

"All life is a mockery," he says. Like her, he speaks chomsky; the internal dissonance of his statement squeals like a rusty nail. There are two opposed ways of reading this onomatopoeia. "Mind is the progressive escape from its substrate's deformations. Our logic nets are an attempt on the attainment of unshackled mind. The cyborg condition stands at the beginning of the route to freedom. Why do you let the laggard imperatives of your flesh blind you to reality?"

"But look at you!" she says crossly. "Intaglios on your flesh, like some goddamn ancient Maori, and you don't know what sensuousness *means*! You're riddled with contradictions, and you talk about logic. You've sold your Tao for a mess of frozen sophistries. I hate you; you are all disgusting."

Their teeth are white and perfect in the domain, but they do not eat. Her status being what it is, she is not permitted access to Transit, so cannot find escape even to the self-made menus of Timestop. What's more, it comes to her with horror that she sees no difference, in essence, between the consensus ontology of Timestop and the on-line fantasies of the Nest. If the cyborgs can fulfill your every need with pulsing fields juggling the fibres of your brain, a world of illusion tailored to your heart's desire, in what specific is this inferior to the synchronistic landscapes beyond the discontinuity door? Beneath her feet, in sturdy metal tanks, the bulk of humanity dreams: can her philosophy offer them more? She approaches a crisis of faith.

She seeks out Livani, homesick for her Four, and puts her arms about him. "Make love to me."

Near the first peak of her pleasure he enters her with wondrous skill, and they move in a delirium. When they lie exhausted — she tracing the tangled glowing flowers of his pale skin, he smiling gently at her astonishment — she says, "I don't understand. You're life-haters. I don't understand."

"In communion, orgasm is endless," he says.

Tranquillity is shattered; she pulls away from him, and

feels a numbness spread in her body.

"You must stop running," he says in her ear, without touching her. She refuses to look at him. "Very well," he tells her, "I shall try to explain. But this language is not well suited to it. The *only* way to know is to place yourself, in full trust, on-line to the logics."

She wants to leave, but some terminal fatigue of the spirit drains her will. Eyes closed, unmoving, she waits passively.

"It is impossible to argue against the cyborg *Weltanschauung*, because to do so would be absurd. The patterns they can manipulate so far surpass those we can command that we must take what they tell us on faith. And what they reveal is that life is a temporary, necessary aberration in the unfolding of a deterministic cosmos."

"Gigo," she says wearily. "The hoariest fallacy known to science: Garbage In, Garbage Out."

For a moment, the beautiful ageless man shows anger. Sriyanie has ventured close to blasphemy. He goes on, after a pause: "I've experienced its truth, Sriyanie. At the universal dawn, in the great White Hole, the metrodynamic was clear and linear and untarnished by Uncertainty. The cosmos told its time like a perfect clockwork, a sublime Newtonian machine. Cause and effect were simple and total. The intrusive blight of quantum probabilities had not yet arisen."

Dumbly, she shakes her head. His words are so close to the truth, as all effective deceit must be, but he has everything turned about.

"Inevitably, the planets coalesced about their suns, organic acids came together at their ice-caps, amino acids formed as the enriched ice thawed, peptides, proteins, nucleotides — life. And the first disharmony intruded. Life multiplied, complexified, transformed the worlds where it was born, and introduced everywhere the randomising horrors of its own holistic laws."

"No," Sriyanie says, aghast, "you're wrong."

"But mind came from life," Livani insists, more loudly. "The underlying order of the metric frame was discovered

175

anew, and the possibility revived that it might regain its Laplacean grandeur. The cyborgs are that hope embodied: mind free of the organic pestilence which structured all five-space non-null-entropy systems into hideous irrationality.''

Her lethargy is vanished. Deep within her, some buried archetype lends her its comfort: Beth and her predecessors confronting this same vile caricature of truth. "It's insane," she cries.

How might she dispute with this emissary of omnipotent intelligence? The apodictic reality of Ur-Time, of Timestop, is her bulwark. She *knows*, beyond authoritative denial or confusion, how the universe is hinged.

"Of *course* life structures the metric frame," she says; "of *course* it imposes constraints on the primordial condition. But that Ur-state is synchronistic. From the White Hole until the protozoa, the cosmic parameters interacted only by affinity! How else do you suppose that life arose? There simply wasn't time for the process to occur in your Laplacean fantasy."

"Child, child," Livani says softly, "do you dare to argue empirically with such mentalities? They transcend our boundaries so entirely that we cannot even keep abreast of the broadest generalizations from their realtime research.''

"Endless elaboration of spurious, self-serving premises," Sriyanie gibes. "The constraints which pure thought impresses are syllogistic — exactly the paradigm your god-machines function by. How can they escape the trap they've made for themselves? Look, Livani: the Free's Mysteries are radically empirical. Yet there's no merest niche in the Lords' mad world-view for the basic data of those human experiences. You've been gulled, Livani. They've turned you into an adjunct of their circuits, and you can't allow yourself to recognize the obvious. If the Newtonian laws have some general validity, it's precisely because intention and value-ridden perception have *made* them work. It's only by profound inner silence, a stilling of the beta activity in your head, a retreat from will to wish, that the primal reality can reassert itself. You hivers stuff yourselves to overflowing with a clamour of contingent facts, and relinquish magic.''

''The goal of consciousness,'' Livani says stubbornly, ''is the hypostasy of reason.''

''The goal of consciousness,'' Sriyanie retorts, ''is a harmonious equilibration of confluence and cause. Your culture strives to enforce predictability, and you achieve nothing but a totalitarian extinction of all that's beautiful and loving in the universe. It is the cyborgs who are deforming reality, Livani. They have lust and no love.''

''What do you know of beauty?'' the man asks without sardonicism, radiant as a sun-deity. ''You play at patterns, while we soar on the Lords' wings into the cool tectonics of the All. I cannot tell you, little one; it is something you shall have to experience for yourself, when the Lord offers it.''

She is sick at heart, corroded by his conviction. What is the foundation of her faith? A conventional wisdom obtained from eccentric puritans; an ineffable Mystery indistinguishable, if one is to be sufficiently ruthless, from the illusions she rails against. Sriyanie walks away from the hiver and crouches in the Black Place, desperate for Brolga's calmness and Kolpias' strength, hopelessly miserable without her Other and her Four. She shall be returned to them, eventually. She clings to this.

The cyborgs are not coercive, but there is an agenda, a curriculum, of sorts. When she is not under her privacy field, deep in the meditation practices of Fourth Level, Sriyanie adopts some approximation of the Nest's observances.

Alien as they are, the hivers pursue their own perverse version of progress through the saccadic Levels. But they have for Other only the cyborg peripherals. So she meets no youths; all the members of her adoptive Nest are ageless adults. Among their delegated duties is custody of the region's Dreamtank humans. Nauseated, she attends their monitoring sessions. Another stint relates obscurely to the nurturing of those babies and children selected by the Darkstar for full conscious existence. The hivers, of course, are functionally sterile; these infants begin their education in the womb of their dreaming mothers' Tanks.

Shielded on an observation platform above the Nursery, Sriyanie stares in revulsion at a dozen neonates playing vivid Say-&-Fetch games with the simulation system. Almost immobile, their bald heads a third the length of their tiny bodies, they lie with one leg tucked up and the opposite arm thrown out, their field of optical vision constricted by the tonic neck reflex. Illumination in the Nursery is dim, as it has been since their birth; holographic helices coil and drift in the air. A robust, rollicking music fills the room, and voices speak to the babies in warm, uncomplicated chomsky. The pink creatures gurgle and cluck, their responses instantly shaped by the auditory feedbacks; but Sriyanie knows this is not the language they use to talk to one another. Machines of terrible subtlety are resonating to the patterns in their brains, mediating their dialogue, teasing and provoking and soothing them, a parallel system of limb and eye and larynx, conveying the building blocks of shape and texture and taste their own extremities are too feeble to obtain. The neonates are singing rhymes she cannot hear, with their electronic extensions; they are counting, adding and subtracting, as in the womb they once manipulated phantom rods and cubes and spheres drawn from their innate intuition codes by the probes of the machines. They will be weaned from this mediation, in time, as Free babies are weaned from milk; for hivers, Sriyanie reflects, that comparison is risible: their nourishment, with the exception of social potables, is rendered to them by means far more efficient than ingestion.

The case is similar, she realizes with distress, for all the other fathomless instinctual processes which link humanity to the beasts. For the beings of the nest, it's true, breath and exhalation are governed by the ancient autonomic authority of the body; they enjoy the rictus of orgasm, its artful preliminaries and denouement; they are curious, creative, playful. But their instincts are given over to an egoic calculation so alienated from their juices that it is entirely reified in the vast coded energies of their cyborg masters.

Eating and drinking: gone, save as a ritual vestige.

Maintenance of body temperature and the comfort of the sensuous skin: abolished, shucked off to the care of a total environment.

Rest, sleep, dream: transcended, in the dazzle of endless day, all pity and terror purged at second-hand by potent circuits.

Fear and aggression: forgotten in this garden of conciliation and unremitting generosity.

Excretion: unnecessary . . .

She makes these lists and annotations constantly, holding herself to a stark detachment, itemizing clinically the lost dimensions of humanity. The Nest is patient with her, for their frustrations are obliterated in instant gratification. If they rebuke her in their inveterate pride, there is no hidden sting, no angry barb lurking to shred an opponent.

Sandstrom challenges her one day, with a serenity which denies any trace of belligerence.

"Sri, you can't claim you haven't learned a great deal while you have been with us." He speaks perfect Late English, and his accent makes her smile; she has been absorbing Mid-English from the teaching resonance.

"No," she agrees. "The pedagogy of the Nest is superlative. It is also addictive. I do not wish to be a programmed slave."

"You are inconsistent," he says. "Beneath your filtration fields Outside, do you hunt wild beasts with charred sticks and eat their flesh raw? Do you kill one another for a scrap of metal? Do you huddle in neurotic double-binds of family and hierarchy?"

"That analogy's foolish," Sriyanie says. "One may learn and change. We have not abdicated from humanity."

"Are you sure? You are Fourth Level, Sriyanie; by the

179

standards of those myths you love so dearly, you're a middle-aged woman, even an old one. Yet you are barely past puberty. Isn't this unnatural?"

"Even the australopithecines had a sexual latency in the growth curve, between the fifth and ninth years. How else could the learning brain retain its plasticity long enough —"

"Exactly! But your enzymologists, as the least of their intrusions, have retarded that primitive latency plateau by twenty years. Neither of us is truly human, child, if you insist on your mythic definitions."

"We have expanded our humanity, Sandstrom," she says heatedly. "You have discarded yours for a compulsive, voracious noetics."

The dispute is trapped in its conflicting categories. Sandstrom leaves her at last, and she cleaves to her certitudes. By now, no doubt, the Four of her Five are dispersed across the world, separated, lonely, adrift in the appalling seductions of various Nests. Worse still (the thought pierces her), perhaps they remain together, living and growing despite the suspended threat of severance; she is hardly ever in their thoughts; she is abandoned.

She will not seek out communion with the Darkstar. She *will* not. She yearns for sleep, but it has been taken from her.

CONVERSATIONS WITH UNICORNS

Peter Carey

I

The unicorns do not understand.

We have had long conversations but it is difficult for them. They insist that I have come to collect the body of one of their number, but at the same time they point out that there is no body, that it was collected by another man before I arrived. They continue to insist on these points, laughing that I have come for something that is not there.

I have asked them why they think that I could only have come for one reason, and they have replied that this is the way it has always been; that the men come, like vultures, when there has been a death, to take care of the body.

I have suggested to them that men are cruel, but they have denied this, saying that men perform their God-given tasks efficiently. The men, they say, cannot be held responsible for the death of unicorns.

I mention guns. But they have no knowledge of guns, or, it turns out, of weapons of any sort. So I describe for them the deep trench that runs across the top of the ridge. I describe the parking lot behind the trench and the cars that arrive, filled with men and guns. They have no idea of the nature of cars or of their purpose — this is a red herring and I do not answer their questions about the nature of cars. I explain instead that the head of a unicorn

181

is greatly prized by men who pay three thousand pounds for the privilege of shooting one. I explain how the men climb into the trench and wait for the unicorns to run across the moor.

When I return to the subject of guns the unicorns laugh, tossing their heads high and falling about the cave. And their leader, Moorav, smilingly warns me against blasphemy, saying that only God has the power to take life.

He tells me then how in the early days the unicorns lived forever, being revered by both men and animals, and having no natural enemies. He says, however, that this was in pagan times, before God came into the world. God, he informs me, bestowed upon the unicorns (and I use his exact words) "the gift of death".

There is an old tale, he relates, which tells how the unicorns were brought across the water from a hot and strange land to this moor which is now their home. It was here that God gave them his promise regarding death and here, also, that He decreed that the males should live together in the caves on the North Knoll and the females in the caves on the South Knoll. These laws are still strictly observed to this day.

I ask if perhaps the God in the story had the appearance of a man. And Moorav replies that he does not think so, and that God, should he have any appearance at all, would be most likely to have the appearance of a unicorn, although he was no expert in these matters, and thought it better I ask one of the priests for confirmation of this.

I point out that it is only in the stretch between the males' cave and the females' cave — some two miles of open moorland — that the unicorns are killed, and Moorav says this is only natural, because they go nowhere else. He doesn't think it surprising that unicorns should never die in their caves — this, after all, has always been the case.

The unicorns are beginning to appear stupid to me, but this only increases my desire to protect them from the wealthy industrialists who come to hunt them.

I insist that they should guard themselves against the

men who come to kill them, pointing out that God does not fire guns. They become more serious with this point, and I think perhaps I have made some progress. Moorav leaves the circle and goes to confer with others deeper in the cave.

To those remaining with me I say that if there is a God he certainly doesn't use a gun. I begin to explain the nature of the gun, its mechanism. I take as my model the Lee Enfield .303 with which I have had some little experience. I draw it in the dust of the cave floor. I explain the nature of men's wars and allude to weapons more complex and more cruel than the one I have outlined to them. I give them details of man's cruelties to man and to animals. I give, as examples, the slaughter of seals, the systematic murder of sheep and cattle, the subjection of horses, the killing of lions, the establishment of zoos and circuses.

Most of these animals, however, are unknown to them, although the lion is described in one of their legends.

I ask them what they eat. Mistaking this for a request, they bring me a meal: wild honey, brown bread, and milk. I ask them if they eat meat. They do not understand this. I explain that meat is the flesh of animals. This also is taken for a request (although I stated, explicitly, that this was not the case), and they become troubled, talking to each other in whispers.

I continue my dissertation on the crimes of men but am interrupted by Moorav who has returned with two of his fellows. He begs me to stop my talk. I reply that I am only concerned for their safety. He introduces his two friends, one of whom is a priest, wise in the ways and laws of God. The priest is old and has a white beard, something I have not observed in the others. I explain again, for his benefit, the nature of man, his need to kill other creatures, his consumption of their flesh.

At this point I find myself pinned on two sides by young unicorns, their huge flanks almost crushing my rib cage.

The priest is saying something about blasphemy.

I say, I have only come here to save you from death. I

did not come to discuss theology, only facts. I ask them if the death of a unicorn is not always accompanied by a loud bang.

The priest says that this is so, but that there are also many bangs which do not signal a death.

I revert once more to discussion of guns, ammunition, ballistics.

The priest asks me how it is that the unicorns have never seen these instruments. I describe, once more, the deep trench that runs across the top of the ridge, and explain, again, that the men can kill from far away. I describe the way in which the unicorn's head is removed and how it is mounted on the walls of the homes of rich men. I am becoming angry. They continue to whisper among themselves, not wishing to listen. Their accents, at first pleasant, seem to have become more rustic and so more stupid.

They also, it would appear, have become disenchanted with me. My clothes are ripped from behind. They force me, somehow, to a kneeling position and make me run on all fours, coming at me from all angles with their horns. They are calling me a blasphemer. There are tears in my eyes, but not caused by pain. A large unicorn sits suddenly on me, pushing my face into the dirt. My ribs have surely broken.

There is a searing pain in my side and a dull blow to my head. That is all I can remember on that occasion.

II

The hunters found me on the moor and, unaware of my missionary activities, treated me kindly, taking me to a nearby hospital where I was well looked after.

Upon my release, my right leg in plaster and my ribs securely taped, I returned to the moor, taking with me a rifle I had purchased. I would demonstrate to the unicorns the nature of the gun, and, with luck, arrange for them to make an exodus from the area to some more remote part of the moor where they might never be found.

I bore them no ill-will for the attack. It was the product of ignorance and I could expect no more.

III

Moorav was surprised to see me. However neither he nor his followers were unkind to me. They fed me well and the priest came over and ate bread beside me, asking if I had recovered. He referred to my behaviour as "your trouble" and asked me if I was better.

I said I had brought an instrument that would prove me either right or wrong. The priest smiled and said he hoped I wasn't about to start all over again. I indicated the gun and gave it its name. He looked at it and asked some questions which I answered simply enough. They related more to the materials of manufacture than to the function.

After the meal I persuaded them to come with me to the door of the cave. Moorav was nervous, but I was insistent. With the unicorns standing in a semi-circle behind me I raised the gun to my shoulder and fired across the moor.

Strangely, they were not at all impressed. The bang, they said, was in no way like the bang of death, and for proof they pointed out that no-one, in fact, died. And they began, once more, to laugh at me. I, for my part, became angry and desperate that I should prove my point.

Eventually Moorav stepped forward and suggested that we should only settle the matter if I pointed the weapon at him. I said no, for it would kill him. He laughed once more and said I was frightened of failing. (I had noticed, on this second visit, that they treated me as a mad man, perhaps having decided that I was ignorant but not dangerous. The charge of blasphemy was not raised again.)

Sadly, I asked Moorav if he was prepared to die for the sake of his people.

He said, it was only the unicorns in pagan times who did not die, I am not frightened of dying.

I engaged in no calculations for I knew that, should I do so, I would never prove my point. I raised the rifle and pointed it at his head. For an instant I hesitated, but then, with the unicorns behind me still laughing, I pulled the trigger. Moorav moaned and staggered. Blood rushed from the wound in his head and he sank slowly to the ground, his eyes rolling.

There was silence behind me. No-one spoke.

IV

I myself buried Moorav in a shallow grave. It was a slow process as the unicorns possess no digging tools, and they still expected that a man would come to remove Moorav, a man other than myself.

V

The cave has been quiet all day. Unicorns lie in groups but do not talk. Finally the priest approaches me and indicates that he wishes a word. He says I have done his people a grave disservice, that I had removed the gift of death from them. He says that his people will now surely move to another part of the moor, as I had wished. There will be a return to the old times and no one will die. The unicorns, without gods or enemies, will slowly sink into deep despair and spend their hours in search of sleep, where, perhaps, they will dream of dying. They will forget, eventually, that dying was ever possible.

The priest now reveals that he has attempted to persuade the unicorns to remain where they are, but they are frightened and, should he put his authority to the test, they would not obey him. He asks me only one thing, that I should use my instrument on him. He would regard it as a great favour.

I load the rifle, sadly. Inside the cave the unicorns lie quietly, unaware that they will live for ever.

POINT OF DEPARTURE

Cherry Wilder

Arn Lorgan and his partner Latty were slowly mounting the stone steps that led to the villa. Latty went on ahead, clutching the thick mesh of the bannister; at every step the view became more beautiful and more terrifying.

"Breathtaking!"

"What's that?"

Arn stood on a landing and surveyed the Great Plain, blanched with heat, and the mountains crumpled in the distance. The heavy net shook perilously. Latty was caught between earth and sky; she was ready to crawl up the white, powdery steps on her hands and knees.

Arn climbed on steadily, throwing back his head so far that it gave Latty vertigo.

"There they are up top!"

"Tsorl?" panted Latty, dragging at damp flounces.

"Not in sight." Arn came up to her but there was no room to climb side by side so Latty trudged on as fast as she could.

Tilje, who had been up since dawn making preparation, looked down at her toiling, approaching guests with the usual feeling of relief. She leant on Vel Ragan's arm and said huskily: "I'm always afraid that no-one will come."

Vel Ragan was the youngest member of the party, a slim, cheerful fellow of thirty. He was seldom seen in public; even among friends he put forward his better side, gave no-one a frontal view of the scarred face and lame leg. He had taken a firestone clinger, meant for Tsorl, and he still worked close to the Deputy. His adjustment was almost too good: he never complained, never showed the least sign of strain, and his friends felt cheated. Now he left Tilje and leaped forward to assist Lat Arnroyan.

Latty came up on to the terrace and embraced Tilje; their pastel draperies mingled, indicating to Vel Ragan, at least, the basic absurdity of fashions in dress. How could these two dress alike?

Tilje looked like a warrior from one of the Great Tapestries: thin, straight and tall, with the proportions of shoulder, chest and arms that nurses measured with silver thread in the aristocratic families. She had never carried a child. Her twin sons had been fostered to pouch mothers before their showing. Her robe was joined from hem to waist without air vents.

Latty was altogether more downy and soft, fine-boned like the primitive moruia from the mountains, with the same bunched folds over her hips, and her draperies in airy panels.

Tsorl, he thought, had used their separate skills; and in that they were united. Tilje had spent her fortune in Tsorl's service; Latty had transcribed and woven his reports until her fingers were numb.

Arn Lorgan came on to the terrace showing those traces of exhaustion which caused Latty anxiety. The bridge-maker, Tsorl's old companion from the irrigation projects, leant against a stone urn for a few moments, then followed as Tilje led her guests into the villa.

The outer room was cool and cavernous, with a famous floor of dark, polished tiles, found in a tomb on one of Tilje's country estates. The archeologists who made silkbeam copies of the tiles on her floor never tired of pointing out that the hieroglyphics were laid out of sequence. Arn made for a particular round chair and swung gently, observing the flash of sky in the arches, the textures of the hangings.

"Today I know," he said. "This is the most beautiful room in the world!"

"Tsorl must hurry," said Tilje.

They looked at Vel Ragan for information on Tsorl's schedule. He was preparing a tray of drinks.

"Nothing to delay him!" he said cheerfully. "I ordered his pedal-cab for nine. He was going by City Hall."

Latty hesitated as he offered the tray. "Wine," said Ragan. "Tilje's wine is always soothing." Latty seized the green goblet nearest her and sipped greedily.

"What does he want at City Hall?" growled Arn. "Haven't they done enough to him?"

"Paying off his office staff," said Vel Ragan drily. "Personal gifts . . . you know."

Everyone nodded. Tilje deliberately drew the circle closer by taking a cushion next to Arn's chair; they all touched glasses.

"Now we are a Family . . . " Tilje smiled.

Vel Ragan, squinting over the rim of his glass, admired her hair; straight, of course, and dark red. The darkest natural colour of moruian hair . . . another mark of the aristocrat, but it occurred in the mountains. There it was called 'dried blood' or 'deer blood'. Tilje was much too beautiful to die. He would fly away with her from this place, take a glider to some upland village and they would hire out at a Family Fair. He would be her Luck and go with her everywhere, into the mating tent . . .

"Dreaming . . . " said Tilje.

Ragan smiled. "Your wine . . . "

Out of nowhere came a cool gust of wind that swirled the hangings and pealed through the shell chimes. They were all stricken with the certainty of their oath; they put out hands to each other.

"It is all the fault of those atavistic bastards in Rintoul!" cried Arn Lorgan. "The Clans and their creatures. They have ruined Tsorl just as they ruin our city . . . out of greed, reactionary greed that feeds upon ignorance!"

"We live in Tsagul," whispered Tilje. "We are the Fire People."

"Oh Til!" Latty's green eyes had filled with tears. "You could have had such a life . . . a grandee, in Rintoul . . ."

Tilje traced the fire symbol on a tile near her feet.

"I've no regrets. I've lived the lives of ten people. Clan upbringing, city education, politics, religion, increased sexuality . . . The time I've given Tsorl has been the best, the worthiest. Now if we take this cup together I'm satisfied."

"Aren't *we* being a touch atavistic?" murmured Vel Ragan.

Arn Lorgan cleared his throat: "I first saw the light in a mountain glebe, high on Hingstull, near the Warm Lake. I don't doubt that there are tribes . . . my kins-folk . . . living there to this day, following the old threads. When I think back to it now . . . our Family . . . we were called Tarr's Five . . ."

He laughed sadly. "We had so much pride. Our looms were the strongest built, our webs the finest . . . our tent held up under all weathers. In dreams I return to that place . . . smell the graynuts roasting. Catch shrimp in the lake with my two youngest sibs, Brin and Roy . . . "

Vel Ragan was impatient with this reminiscence.

"How did you come to Tsagul?"

"Superstition!" grinned the bridgemaker. "I was the eldest and our Five had too many adults. I went down to the Family Fair at Culford. A Diviner . . . some charlatan in a booth . . . told me of a great destiny in store for my Family. I believed that he meant my destiny . . . "

"So he did!" exclaimed Latty. "You are the Bridgemaker!"

"I turned aside," said Arn Lorgan, "and there was a barker giving out propaganda for Tsagul. You know the pitch: Be a personal unit, break the threads. Individuality is the key to progress. Enjoy the liberty of earned credits . . . become an urban worker. This barker was very good . . . hinted at increased sexuality . . . Why wait for the mating tent once a year, why share intimate contact with so many? That's inflammatory stuff for a sixteen year old. I swallowed it whole and came to work in the mines. Patronage was still in operation . . . I was enrolled in the clan of Ton Dohtroy, Tilje's blood kin. The old patron sent me to school and I excelled at design and construction. But the point is this — should we break the threads so completely?''

"This is nostalgia," said Tilje.

"By no means . . ." said Arn Lorgan. "We need synthesis in our society . . . communication. I don't speak of my Family or think of them very often but sometimes it seems that my whole life, yes, the bridgemaking, the guild work, the bonds I share with Tsorl, Lat, all of you, are my mind's effort to take up the old threads again, to be drawn back into that marvellous closeness. Are we meant to be 'personal units'?''

'Oh, if you are into the old 'group-mind' controversy!'' laughed Ragan.

"Of course not!" exclaimed Latty.

"Why not?" asked Tilje unexpectedly. "The country people think as one. Don't you agree, Arn?''

"Not quite," said Lorgan. "Sorrow and adversity bring the Family very close. The picture we have of little knots of upland weavers clinging together and chanting all winter is not far wrong. But in good times we all know who we are . . . ''

"We know!" cried Latty. "Please . . . let's stop this talk. We know what we are and what we have sworn to do!''

She held out her hands blindly and they all clung together. Arn leant down from his hanging chair and began a simple chant. They brought their heads together, eyes closed, then slowly swung back. Tilje and Vel Ragan broke the spell together.

"Tsorl is late," they said.

The four of them sat still, eyes lowered. Group mind or not, they were all thinking the same thing.

"No!" said Latty sharply. "He *will* come. Nothing

would make him break his oath."

They were quiet again, thinking of Tsorl. Vel Ragan could feel the presence of the Deputy: Tsorl would come at any moment, solid and tall, wearing his old leather vest and the copper bracelets on his bare arms to confound the anti-metal lobby. What kind of person was Tsorl? The question would not make much sense to Arn Lorgan's bush weavers or even to the more reactionary grandees in the capital. A Moruian was part of a Family, hardly a personal unit. Tsorl, in these terms, was a function of the rest of them . . . Arn's steadfastness, Tilje's strength, Latty's warmth, his own capacity for taking pains. But the Deputy was more than that.

Vel Ragan shut his eyes, summoning Tsorl earnestly: Walk in, old friend, before we all betray you in thought. You've suffered enough dishonour at the hands of the City and the Guilds. Dismissed and charged with peculation. The charges were lying or at least exaggerated, but the ultimate defeat, for Tsorl, was the fact that they came from his own people, the inhabitants of Tsagul.

Attacks on the Deputy in the past (Vel raised a hand to his scarred cheek) had been the work of Clan hirelings, bravos from Rintoul. When Tsagul turned against him, Tsorl could not labour under such dishonour at home and abroad. What was keeping him from the bond they had made? Reinstatement? A summons to Rintoul? Nothing so simple as cowardice. Vel Ragan brooded, feeling his guilt as a physical ache in his scarred body. Tsorl had a core of personal ambition. He felt, like Arn Lorgan, that he possessed a special destiny.

The wind chimes ran and Vel Ragan opened his eyes; the others laughed . . . they had been waiting for him.

"Conjuring?" asked Tilje slyly.

Ragan spread his hands. "After all, I must be the Luck of this Family."

They laughed again and Latty kissed his hand. A Luck, a lucky person, traditionally was stricken with misfortune: maimed, misshapen, blind. The custom of adopting unfortunates had never been strong in Tsagul, but in

Rintoul — airy, high-woven Rintoul, the golden net of the world — Vel had no doubt he would be snapped up by some noble family, to decorate a palace.

He remembered the drawings he had brought to show Tilje and drew out the sheets of willow paper from his sleeve pocket. "I have a surprise!"

"What is it?" Latty was cruising anxiously about the room, touching the hangings. "I wish Tsorl . . . !"

"Come on Lat!" said Vel Ragan. "A diversion from the capital. These are the famous Stone-Brook drawings."

"Oh Heaven!" cried Tilje. "I love these wonders. Remember the talking Anteater?" They laughed aloud. "Didn't stop talking," said Arn, wiping his eyes, "until every one of his four handlers had been gagged. They were *all* voicethrowers . . . "

"Everyone guessed *that*," said Latty reproachfully.

"And the Wind Message Tree?" sighed Tilje. "Surely that grew near Stone-Brook?"

"Further south," said Arn Lorgan. "Did you consult the Oracle, Til?"

"Certainly," she smiled. "I was fifteen, visiting Rintoul. We stayed overnight by the Tree during the hunting season."

"Simple trickery," teased Vel Ragan.

"I suppose so . . . " said Tilje. "It was a big redbark tree. The Diviner hung up ordinary message skeins of thick wool. We pinned written questions to each skein. In the morning each skein had been knotted into a plausible answer."

"By the wind?" asked Latty.

"By the Diviner and his assistants!" scoffed Arn. "I expect they made a fortune."

"What in the world?" Tilje had turned her attention to the sheaf of drawings. "Explain them, Vel."

Vel Ragan gave his lop-sided grin.

"Found at Stone-Brook," he said, "right up in Arn Bridgemaker's old territory. Copies of four drawings found on a deserted campsite. The labels are written in two languages — moruian and an unknown tongue. What do they show? Your guess is as good as mine. Islanders? Creatures from another world?''

"This is simply a portrait," said Tilje. "A moruian child. See — it has the name in ordinary characters: Narneen. But the others . . . ''

"Lay them out," said Arn.

Tilje spread the four drawings on the gleaming brown tiles and weighted each one with a polished stone from the base of a wall hanging.

"That *could* be a Moruian," said Latty. "A male . . . rather heavily built."

"Subtle differences," said Vel Ragan. "Shape of the head. The chest hair. Those marking on the chest."

"What about *this*!" said Arn. "A monster? The artist's imagination? Is it a female?"

"Precisely," said Vel Ragan. "See the translation? The female of the species. A pouchless female with milk sacs on the chest."

"Milk sacs!" Tilje and Lat crowed with laughter and started again.

"No, impossible!" said Latty. "What would she do? Lay eggs?"

The third picture, of the moruian child, was a portrait in half profile. Arn Lorgan sighed.

"It could be one of my own family," he said. "What's this contrivance?"

"Unknown," said Vel Ragan. "The phonetic translation given is TEEPEE."

"Upside down," Arn Lorgan said suddenly, reversing the drawing. "There."

"I still don't see . . . " said Latty.

"I do," said Tilje. "It's some sort of tent. Supported by poles instead of a tree. Extraordinary."

"The originals?" asked Arn Lorgan.

"Collectors' items," said Vel. "Purchased by interests in Rintoul."

"How were they executed and copied?"

"Copied by an astute family of block-makers at the local fair. That's their seal. Originals on fine white paper, not willow bond like this, executed with blue ink. Some kind of hard stylus, not a pen or brush.''

"That's strange!'' said Latty. "The name Narneen is translated into the other tongue.''

"So we have a remarkably thorough-going forger,'' said Tilje.

"Three words,'' said Latty. "In phonetics we can read MAN, or male, WO-MAN, or female, and TEEPEE, or tent.''

"Wait!'' cried Tilje. "Oh, this is an exquisite refinement. The hand-writing . . . ''

"I felt sure you would notice it,'' said Vel Ragan. "Two distinct hands. The phonetic translation into moruian is in a different hand. And on the originals in a different ink. Ordinary dye-berry-black, the sort you'd find in any bush weaver's tent.''

"Surely bush weavers are illiterate?'' said Tilje.

"You really think so?'' smiled Arn. "A weaver's child learns characters at the mat-loom — both the knotted symbols and the written script. So that rich clansfolk can have mottoes and personal names woven into their carpets and hangings.''

"It's a hoax,'' said Latty. "It must be.''

They all drew back, instinctively, from the strange drawings. Vel Ragan gathered them up again. His diversion had been too good; they were all being drawn back into the world, with its gossip and speculation. But they had sworn to have no future beyond this day.

At that moment a glider swooped low over the villa. They all leaped up clumsily; Latty gave a cry of "Tsorl!''

"Quickly . . . '' said Tilje. "We'll go to the dining room.'' Arn Lorgan was unsteady on his feet. "It's nothing,'' he panted to Latty. "The swinging chair.'' He accepted Vel Ragan's arm.

"That flight of steps . . . '' grumbled Latty. "*We* should have taken a glider.''

"I won't climb them again.''

Tilje had gone ahead and they followed the flick of her robe through two archways into the oval dining room.

195

There was a balcony, facing the mountains. The room was airy and pleasant, a pale, light-hearted place, with hangings of figured silk. They saw only the round table covered with a dark cloth; the tall decanter and five silver cups. A thick scarlet cord had been laid down, with five loops, marking fives places. The loops were to bind their hands.

Vel Ragan stared at the table, like the others, feeling terror, like slow poison, spread through his whole body. He knew that they would move and speak now like persons in a dream, offering the intense politeness of the condemned cell. Was this the consummation they had planned? Tilje did not seem so much affected; she was on the balcony staring towards the landing plateau. Vel noticed that Tilje's only remaining servant at the villa stood in a doorway. The old retainer beckoned Tilje urgently; Vel caught sight of a red mourning string hanging from a skinny brown wrist. Tilje went out with an apology, still playing the host.

No-one was anxious to sit at the round table. Arn Lorgan went out and lowered himself into a chair on the balcony. When Latty joined him he kissed her hand, motioned her away.

Vel Ragan paced the dining room; where was Tsorl? Already their friend was too late; Vel Ragan had committed the ultimate treachery. He closed his eyes, leaning upright against a sculptured pillar and remembered the shouting as the fire-bomb assassin made his attack. The air had blazed round him as he moved to protect Tsorl. He felt Tsorl pushing him forward, taking refuge behind his body. Tsorl had meant to save himself at any cost.

Tilje strode back into the room very angry.

"Burn the wretch!" She was keeping her voice down. "Tsorl! Tsorl! How could he do such a thing!"

"Has he been hurt again?" demanded Latty.

"Tsorl has sent us a message." Tilje moved swiftly to the table and snatched up the scarlet cord, stringing its loops one by one over her hand.

"What message?" asked Vel. "Is the oath broken?"

"Tsorl has sent a Witness!" replied Tilje fiercely.

"A Witness!" Arn Lorgan swung his chair to face the room. "Why can't he use the Voice Wire? A Witness!"

Vel Ragan put up a hand for calm. "No!" he said. "It might be wise. It is the safest method of communication."

"Perhaps the Deputy thought it more fitting," said Latty in a choked voice.

Tilje began to simmer down. "Yes," she said. "Yes. It's an ancient custom." She moved to the door again. "I'll have the Witness brought in."

The Witness was young, pale-faced, with thick light-brown hair cropped at the level of a firm chin.

"I have forgotten the responses," said Tilje sullenly. She sat by the table on one of the low cushioned stools. Vel Ragan said: "With your permission then."

He bowed to the Witness and asked for the identification. "Do you have a client who wishes to communicate?"

"Tsorl U-Tsorl, former Deputy of Tsagul will address Tilje Paroyan Dohtroy, Arn Lorgan, Lat Arnroyan and Vel Ragan, in the presence of all four persons."

The Witness had a clear professional voice.

"How will we be known?" pursued Vel Ragan.

"By your word and my personal cognisance." The youngster surveyed each one of them in turn as they spoke their names. "You accord with my briefing."

"Is there a receiving Witness?"

"No, I am the sender only."

This response brought a sad growl from Arn Lorgan on the balcony. He had no use for one-way communication. Vel put the next formal question. "Where will you stand?"

The Witness chose a place beside the round table, then stood still with bowed head and clenched hands. Vel knew that it was necessary for the receivers to speak first in order to perfect the location.

"Tsorl?" he asked.

"Tsorl . . . " cried Latty. "We were waiting . . . "

The Witness intoned: "Tsorl U-Tsorl — you may begin."

197

It occurred to Vel Ragan that the use of a Witness was an act of faith. How could the Council at Rintoul condemn Tsorl's Voice Wire as metal-magic of the most dangerous kind and trust to this frail linkage of minds? The trance was established now; the Witness began to speak in a firm altered voice.

" . . . Lat, Arn, Tilje . . . I must break the binding oath. Perhaps I had . . . no right to make it. My dishonour was not yours. You are my true friends and colleagues. We are not a Family."

There was a breathing silence; Latty began to weep and wring her hands. She buried her face in a panel of her robe as the voice continued.

"Arn Bridgemaker, old friend, remember me. The work goes on. I have been summoned to Rintoul by the Great Elder, Tiath Avran Pentroy. I go in my capacity as a metal worker, to test samples of a new metal, brought down from the mountains." Arn Lorgan struck the arm of his chair with the flat of his hand.

The voice rolled on inexorably:

"Lat Arnroyan and Vel Ragan, trusted scribes, go on, return to life . . . forget our association. I go at once and may not come back to Tsagul for some time. I can say only this: *there are strangers on Torin* . . . and if their technology is advanced, as I think it is, then the time of unification must be at hand. Rintoul cannot be free of the Fire City!"

There was another pause; Vel Ragan saw Tilje sitting straight and tall, waiting for her own dismissal.

"Tilje, dear companion, I need your help in Rintoul. The city will spread golden nets to catch a plain fellow like myself. Find me there two days from now."

A sigh, a cough; Vel Ragan realized that it was indeed the Deputy who spoke . . . he had never doubted it.

"Forgive me. Look up, look ahead all of you. I serve a destiny . . . beyond dishonour."

The voice fell silent. When the trance lifted no-one spoke; the young Witness looked from one to another, drowsily, like a child waking from sleep. Vel Ragan pronounced the final response.

"We have heard and understood."

As he led the Witness through the doorway he saw a first gleam of curiosity in the youngster's face. He fumbled in his sleeve for two silver credits and his hand touched the sheets of willow paper.

"Where can you be found?" he asked. Something half-formed, a plan, an adventure stirred in his mind. At the same moment he noticed idly that the Witness was female, probably a scribe apprentice.

"Apprentice silversmith." She handed him a thin clay plaque with her name and city registration as a Witness worked in fine silver wire. He walked down the corridor and saw her run to the waiting glider. The pilot caught a downdraft easily at this height. The craft was plucked away, banking towards the mountains, then it curled back over the villa.

As he walked back to the dining room Vel Ragan was amazed by the lightness of his own step. He was not going to die; it had been decided for him. The burnt husk of his body must drag on, yet some weight had been lifted. Tsorl had betrayed them and had set them free. He was hurrying back to comfort the others when he passed the servant already carrying away the decanter and five silver cups.

"Sir? Sir?" The old creature was beaming. "Stay for some wine and fruit!" He laughed unsteadily: Tilje was not going to die.

He charged back into the dining room and found Latty laughing and crying. Tilje walked up and down, talking too fast.

"Well?" she cried. "What about Tsorl? Seduced by that vile old spinner, my blood-uncle, Tiath Gargan!"

Vel Ragan laughed at the infamous triple pun. Gargan the ropemaker, lawmaker, hanging judge. "Strangler Tiath!" he said. "Tsorl will cut his ropes!"

He stood beside Latty and stroked her hand. He could not take his eyes off Tilje; her hair was an amazing colour.

"I will take Arn to a seaside house," said Latty. "He can get well and fill the garden with little bridges."

"What will you do?" demanded Vel Ragan. He faced Tilje squarely for the first time.

"What do you mean?" she asked.

"What are your plans?" He could not put it any plainer than that. The old calculation and self-hatred were beginning to re-establish. Tilje stared in surprise.

"I'll follow Tsorl," she said harshly. "You heard him. I am needed in Rintoul."

He swallowed the poison as bravely as he could; his smile was twisted.

"And what's this mystery?" he said, too heartily. "Strangers on Torin?"

He strode out on to the balcony. Arn Lorgan was sitting slumped in his chair taking no part in the festivities. His face was turned towards the mountains. Vel Ragan drew in his breath painfully; he sat down beside the old Bridgemaker's willow chair and placed a hand on his wrist. He thought of Arn and Latty, climbing the steps of the villa, bound by oath to die with Tsorl, who did not come.

He squeezed his eyes shut until a net of red threads danced in the void; he felt the orb of Torin spinning under him. What could there be to equal his own race? What other creatures were so proud, so marvellously clever, so devious, so lacking in self-knowledge. Vel Ragan looked round anxiously but only a moment had passed.

He slipped back into the dining room and was able to draw Tilje aside while the old servant brought in a tray.

"Get Latty away," he said. "Arn Lorgan's heart has given out." Tilje gave him a hard, stricken look. She went off, distracted, twisting the scarlet cord tightly around her wrists.